W9-ARS-155

Praise for Drawing with Whitman

Winner of the 2019 Moonbeam Silver Medal for Pre-Teen Fiction

Readers' Favorite 2020 International Book Awards Honorable Mention Children—Grades 4th–6th

"A sweet middle-grade novel about the power of art."

—*Kirkus Reviews*

"*Drawing with Whitman* is an emotional book from which the reader can learn many things. The story has many morals, such as not giving up in tough situations."

—LitPick

"A powerful story told with compassion and an understanding of the inner depth of an artist."

—Emily-Jane Hills Orford for Readers' Favorite

"*Drawing with Whitman* is a beautifully written, engrossing, and completely relevant novel that just hits the nail on the head in so many different ways."

—Asher Syed for Readers' Favorite

"The story is very well written, with lots of descriptions and captivating, intense scenes, particularly the one in which the car crashes. I would definitely recommend this book."

—Kristen Van Kampen (Teen Reviewer)
for Readers' Favorite

"Overall *Drawing with Whitman* is a marvelous, stellar, and supreme book that will entertain, delight, and charm young readers and even adults! And so I, of course, have to award this book five stars!"

—Red Headed Book Lover

Drawing with Whitman

Drawing with Whitman

SOURLAND MOUNTAIN SERIES BOOK 1

Kristin McGlothlin

This is a work of fiction. Names, characters, organizations, places, events, and incidents are either products of the author's imagination or are used fictitiously.

Published by Bird Upstairs, Seattle
www.birdupstairs.com

Produced by Girl Friday Productions
www.girlfridayproductions.com

Design: Paul Barrett
Development & editorial: Alexander Rigby
Production Editorial: Laura Dailey
Cover illustration: Kristina Swarner

ISBN (hardcover): 978-1-954854-01-7
ISBN (paperback): 978-1-7348802-6-7
ISBN (ebook): 978-1-7348802-7-4

There was a child went forth every day,
And the first object he looked upon and received with wonder or pity or love or dread, that object he became,
And that object became part of him for the day or a certain part of the day . . .

—*Leaves of Grass* by Walt Whitman

Sourland Mountain is in central New Jersey, twenty minutes from the town of Princeton. On top of the mountain sit two neighborhoods. The first neighborhood has similar style homes with well-kept lawns and paved streets. They have plenty of land around them and are buffered by woods. North of it is the Backwoods of Sourland Mountain. The houses there are eclectic and not all of the roads are paved. The homes in this neighborhood back up to the park and wildlife sanctuary named the Sourland Mountain Preserve.

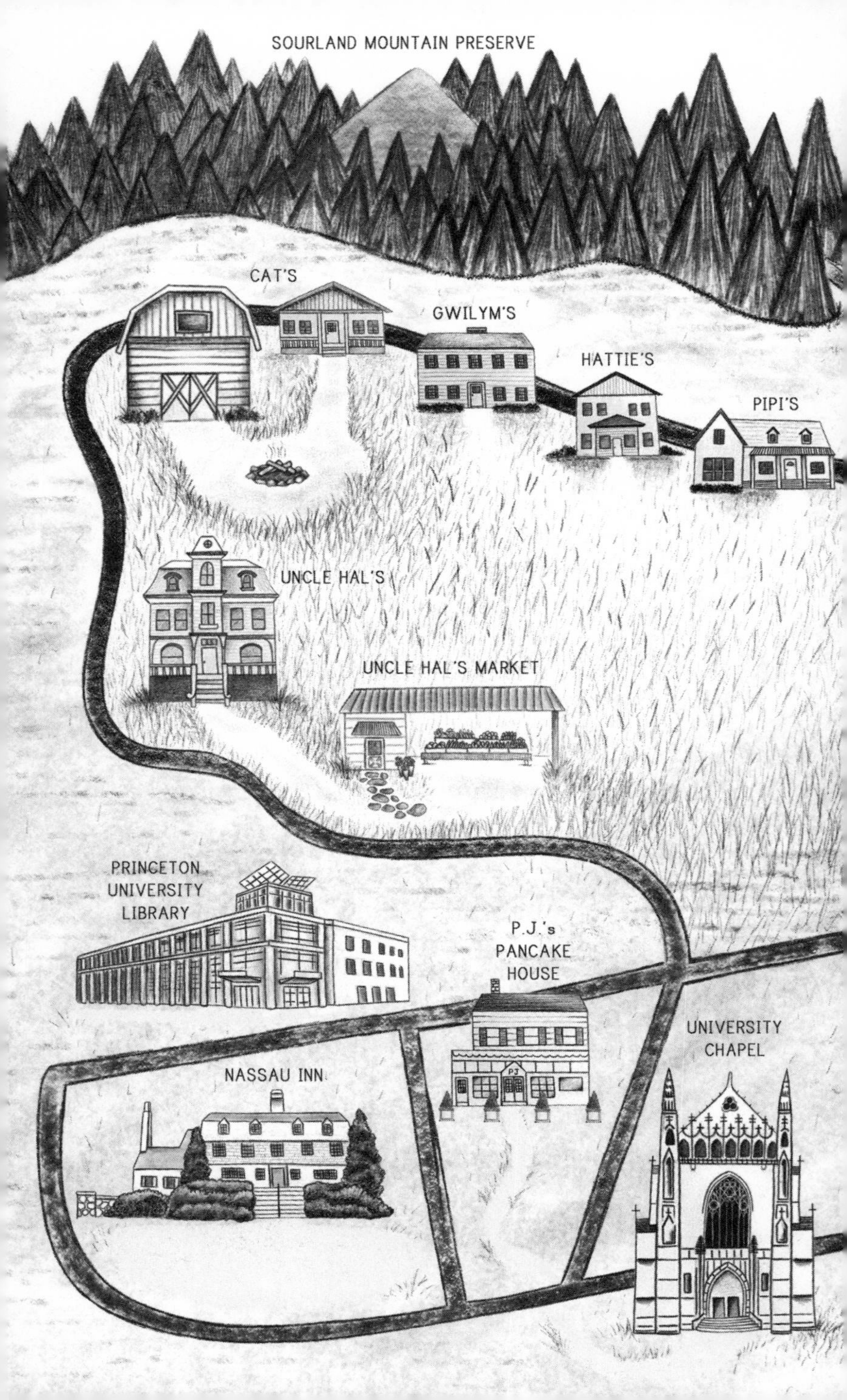
SOURLAND MOUNTAIN PRESERVE
CAT'S
GWILYM'S
HATTIE'S
PIPI'S
UNCLE HAL'S
UNCLE HAL'S MARKET
PRINCETON UNIVERSITY LIBRARY
P.J.'s PANCAKE HOUSE
PJ
UNIVERSITY CHAPEL
NASSAU INN

JOE'S
LIBRARY
LIBRARY
GEORGE'S
RIVER'S
OLD BARN
PARTY
TOOLS
MOVIE
MUSIC
TIGER'S TALE
ART

AUGUST

"Yeah!" screamed Catalynd Jewett Hamilton, running with the football across the field. She stopped and launched it into the fading sunlit sky.

The ball sailed into her brother Buddy's hands. He juked forward and backward, then returned it. They were near the end of their practice.

Catalynd's sandy-brown braid swung into her face as she picked the ball up from the ground. She sliced it sideways to him. Ever since she could catch and throw a football, this had been their weekly routine, to prepare for the annual family Thanksgiving football game.

"I'm going to be the quarterback this year," she informed him.

"Ha! You're dreaming." Buddy laughed. "So, by the way, who's going to throw with you when I'm gone?"

"I don't know. And thanks a lot for leaving me. Why would you want to go to Florida anyway? Hey, are you going to throw the ball?"

He tossed it back. She caught it and returned it, noticing the darkening peach-and-rose-colored sky emerging over the Backwoods of Sourland Mountain.

"Mom's coming. I guess that means you two are going to the store now," he said, walking to their house.

She turned her attention from the evening sky to her mom descending the front steps. Her mom's dark brown bangs blew in the wind. She hoped she would be pretty like her mom.

"We need rain," her mom said, opening the door of their blue Toyota sedan. "Cat, are you ready?"

Cat tied the shoelaces on her red Converse sneakers. "Yes."

"I want to get back in time for my evening walk with your dad."

Her mom was about to back down the driveway when one of the two men who had been watching the scene from the roof of the red barn motioned to them.

"Yes, Hal?" She leaned her head out the window and called to her younger brother. Cat looked at her uncle Hal. His cropped haircut made his head look like a big square, which always made her giggle. Buddy had the same stocky build. Next to him was her dad, with his wild gray hair and tall figure. They had been repairing the barn's roof.

"Be careful," Hal cautioned. "Looks like a storm's coming." To his niece he said, "Cat, don't worry. He's a friend of mine. I've known him for years. Since college." She smiled up at him, but anxiety filled her stomach. *I don't care if he is nice. I still don't want him moving into* my *barn!*

"See you later," Cat's dad said, and waved to them. Her mom nodded at him, then turned to her daughter. "I hope your dad and uncle remembered to fix the latch on the studio-barn door like I asked them to."

They passed her dad's beat-up maroon Range Rover and her uncle's new blue Chevy pickup truck. *Soon there'll be another car, the artist's car.*

"Do you have the grocery list?"

Cat nodded. Her mom paused, then placed her hand on her daughter's leg. "You'll miss throwing the football with Buddy, won't you?"

"I guess." Cat concentrated on her hands. Her mom's recognition of one of her problems didn't make her feel better. She had begun to feel stress, which she hadn't experienced before. It had emerged when Buddy told her that he was going to Florida State University; it increased when the renovation of the barn began. The rent money would help pay for college. *Buddy's moving out and some stranger's moving in. Who is this guy, really?* "Uncle Hal said his name is Benton? Is that his first or last name?"

"Benton Whitman. And as your uncle told you, don't worry. Your dad and I met him. You know we wouldn't have someone live here who we didn't feel comfortable with."

"But what if he's crazy and murders us?"

"That's a bit extreme, Cat." Her mom turned the car onto the road leading into the Backwoods. "Situations change. And usually it's for the best."

"Things don't *have* to change," the girl scoffed.

The evening darkness swelled around their car. Cat watched the patches of light close up. The coming of night comforted her, made her feel safe. She liked leaving the paved road, identical mailboxes, and green lawns of their street and going into the less-tamed neighborhood.

Cat loved the giant, narrow pines that lined one side of the road in the Backwoods and the houses on the other side that were all different styles and sizes. Some were taken care of, and others not so much. She knew them in order. Her two favorite houses were coming up. First was the house she had named the Post-it Note home, a yellow ranch with cream columns and a pool surrounded by white light posts. Cat was positive the people who lived there must be fun. Her second favorite was a two-story with peeling red paint and a wraparound balcony painted light gray. She was convinced it had to be a comfortable place to live.

The car headlights picked up the familiar sight of the big curve cluttered with the guardrail, orange barricades with iridescent white stripes, and three yellow warning signs: one for the sharp curve, another to caution drivers about people riding horses, and the last sign showing the speed limit of fifteen miles per hour. *Fifteen. I'll be fifteen in two years.*

As they passed the road signs, Cat realized no music was playing. "Hey, do you want some tunes?" Her mom nodded. Cat scanned through the list of songs and selected one of their favorites: "Queen of Hearts" by Juice Newton. They belted out the lyrics. Cat imagined them on stage in front of a sea of fans. The rain now falling on the windshield sounded like applause.

"Mid-ni-i-ight . . ."

The rain came down harder, and the wipers fought it off. With wide eyes, Cat watched the buckets of water splash against the glass. She stopped singing. "Mom?" Cat braced her back against the seat and grabbed the door handle as thunder and lightning surrounded them.

Her mom, now humming to the Juice song, answered, "Yes?"

"How far are we from the store?" Cat looked out her window into the night.

"Not far. We're almost to the entrance of the Preserve." The confident tone of her voice suggested to Cat that she was unconcerned about the weather. They drove alongside the Sourland Mountain Preserve.

Cat glanced down into the darkness where her sneakers were. She moved her toes inside them. She wanted to get out of the car but—of course—couldn't. She inhaled and counted to five, then exhaled and tried to push all the breath out of her lungs.

"Some rain," her mom said. Cat was relieved to hear her finally acknowledge the threatening conditions they were in. She noticed her mom stiffen her arms and tighten her grip on the steering wheel. The next Juice song came on. Cat turned the player off.

Cat sensed the car tires losing their grip on the road. Her heart lunged forward as she wished they were home with Buddy and her dad. She was scared, and she realized they were trapped.

As their car swerved to the right, a tree shone in the headlights. It was right in front of Cat. Her mom frantically whipped the steering wheel to the left. The car ignored her actions and continued on its track toward the tree on Cat's side.

No. No. No. No. Consumed with both dread and awe, Cat prepared herself for the crash. Fear grabbed her stomach as she watched their car race toward the thick trunk. She wished it was possible to reverse time.

The impact was like a brick hitting her chest, followed by the sound of the car being crunched. Her leg bones felt as if they flipped back and forth, then split in half, like twigs her dad prepared for one of their bonfires.

Cat was afraid to look at her mom, who remained still and silent. Then she grabbed Cat's shoulder. Her mom's voice barely registered over the sound of the pounding water. "Catalynd, don't move." Cat's head felt like it was full of fog. She heard the click of her mom's seat belt, the car door open. Pain surging up her legs made her wince. She closed her eyes. She recounted the feel of the thud when the car hit the tree. *What's happened? I'm still in the car. Mom. Where's Mom? Oh, I hear her outside on the phone.* Images swirled around her brain. *Rain on the windshield. Wipers swinging back and forth. Headlights shining on grass. A tree trunk . . .*

She felt abandoned. "Mom, my legs. They hurt so bad," she whispered to the empty car.

It didn't take too long for a police vehicle to pull up behind them. Cat watched in the side mirror as her mom walked to the police as they approached the accident. *Why are the flashing blue and red lights on police cars so harsh?*

Within a short time, Cat was squinting at the ambulance lights flashing at her in the mirror. As she was helped out of the car, she fixed her eyes on the paramedics' reflective jackets. The first responders worked at getting her legs out of the car with the rest of her. They placed her onto a stretcher, and her mom grabbed her hand.

❧

Cat's dad and Buddy arrived at the hospital. A nurse checked over her and her mom in the emergency room. Her mom had sustained no visible injuries; Cat obviously had. Her parents and brother stood nearby as two nurses helped Cat from a wheelchair onto the X-ray table. Then she was rolled into a room, where the doctor eventually entered with slides of her legs.

He told them her tibiae were fractured. "To break this bone," he continued, "takes a major force. The casts will go over her knees. It will most likely take four to six months to heal."

He left them. A nurse returned and asked her what color she would like for her casts. "The lime green, please," Cat said with a small smile.

After the leg casts were set, Cat moved the heavy things side to side. *This sucks.*

She was helped into the back seat of her dad's SUV. From the front passenger seat, her mom stretched back to rest her hand on Cat's cast. She held it there the whole way home.

❧

Cat opened her eyes, then moved her legs. The casts were still there. She sighed. She heard murmuring in the kitchen that sounded like her grandma and uncle talking to her parents in quiet, concerned voices. She realized that she couldn't just get up and walk into the kitchen now. Cat slowly rolled onto her side and hugged her pillow.

"Cat?" her mom whispered from the bedroom doorway. "Cat? Are you awake yet?" She sat on the edge of her bed.

"Yes," Cat said. "I'm awake. But I'm not getting out of bed today."

"You have to," her mom said. "You have to get up and get dressed and eat. C'mon." She gently pushed Cat's leg. She knew it was fruitless to ignore her mom. She wouldn't leave until Cat got up. In a way, it was like any other morning, with her mom in her room telling her to rise and shine.

Cat pushed herself up with her hands. "What do I do now?"

Her mom positioned the wheelchair next to the bed and studied it. "I think I lower the side. Like this," she said and released the latch that let the side panel down. Cat slid onto the seat of the wheelchair. Her mom then pulled up the side and clicked it into position. "There we go."

With her mom's help, she moved each leg with its heavy lime-green cast onto a leg rest. The wheelchair appeared gigantic. "How am I ever going to move this monster around?"

"Practice," answered her mom. She backed up the wheelchair to the door.

"I feel gross too," she said, scrunching up her shoulders.

"I'm sure you do. We'll figure how to get you into the tub after breakfast. One thing at a time. We'll get it down to a routine." A wave of appreciation swept over Cat. Her mom would take care of her.

Cat was chilly and motioned to her mom to get the sweatshirt draped over her desk chair. Once she had it on, it warmed her up. Her mom pulled socks halfway up her feet to cover her toes. Cat breathed in.

"There. Now we're ready." She looked at Cat's expression. "I'm sorry. I know it's no fun, I know. But you're tough. You'll make it through this. You'll be proud of yourself for getting through this."

Yeah, but when, and what if I don't get through this, and I'm afraid I won't be normal again. And when was the last time I ate something? Cat's stomach rumbled.

Her mom rolled her into the room where the family sat around the kitchen table. Her family looked at her with concerned eyes. Cat's cheeks heated up. She was embarrassed to be the focus of attention. *I must look frightful in these leg casts and this gigantic wheelchair.*

"Hey, honey." Her dad came and kissed the top of her head.

"Hey, how are you feeling?" asked Buddy. He moved his chair to a corner so Cat could be at the table. Then he realized that she couldn't with her legs sticking out in front of her. "Oh. That won't work."

"Maybe you can . . . Hm." Her mom moved Cat's wheelchair alongside the table. It took up the whole side of the table so only two people could sit. Her mom ignored this and said, "I think you lock the wheels like this."

"Mom," Cat said. "I'm taking up too much space. Just put me against the wall, then you guys have enough room to sit at the table." Her mom took her suggestion, but now Cat felt like she was in a high chair, sitting away from the table. "How am I going to eat?"

"Thought of that," said her dad, smiling. "This TV tray should elevate high enough to slide over your lap." It worked. "And I made you pancakes." He put a stack in front of her.

Cat cheered. "Thanks, Dad. Yum." She plowed a big piece into her mouth and smiled.

Uncle Hal, standing next to the counter, came over and patted her shoulder. "Hey, champ. I broke my leg falling from a tree. I had to use crutches. It was no fun." Cat grinned at him, but thought, *Yes, it's no fun—but* you *didn't have to be in this hideous wheelchair.*

Her grandma walked over and patted her arm. "How are you, my dear?"

"I'm okay, Grandma. I don't think I'm going to be any good at this wheelchair, though."

She put her hand on the padded gray armrest. It was cracked at the seams.

"You'll get the hang of it," said Uncle Hal. "I just wanted to check in on you two. Gotta go. Veggies call." Her uncle had an organic farm and a market at the edge of the property, which were very popular on the weekends.

"I should be going too," said her grandma. "If you need anything, just call." She paused and looked at Cat's wheelchair. "What are you going to do with Cat, now that she's stuck in a wheelchair?" Cat wondered what her grandparent meant. "She can't possibly go on the trip to Florida in her condition." *Oh, the drive to Tallahassee. I'd forgotten.* Her heart sank.

"Yes," agreed her dad. "We were going to ask you if you could stay here with her while we're gone." Standing next to Cat, he placed his hands on her shoulders.

"Of course," she said.

Buddy left the room too, saying something about all the things he still needed to do.

"Now," began Cat's mom. She sat at the table with a notepad and pen. "I started a list of things we need and things we need to do. Your uncle Hal said he'd build a ramp for the front door. Will you grab the pamphlet on the bathroom accommodations?" She motioned to Cat's dad.

"Sure, hon." He picked them up from the kitchen countertop and handed them to her.

"Can I have one too?" Cat asked. It was one of bathroom tips. *Ugh.*

Cat's chest caved in. She didn't want her daily routine changed, especially *that* routine! Already she wasn't able to sit at the table like the rest of her family. Also, last night at the hospital, she'd listened to her mom ask her dad what insurance would cover. Then at the medical supply store, her mom had gasped when the salesman told them the price of renting a wheelchair for six months. *So I'm helpless and a burden.*

. . . and now, the fiasco of the bathroom. Just to get the wheelchair from her bedroom to the kitchen had been more of a challenge than Cat had realized. The metal wheels next to the rubber ones didn't move so easily. It was hard to steer the chair in the direction she wanted to go. Her mom had struggled to turn the wheelchair around in the hallway and finally realized it was impossible to do. The method they settled on was to back the wheelchair out of Cat's bedroom, then veer to the right or left, depending on whether Cat was going to the bathroom or the kitchen, family room, or front door.

Cat looked at the bathroom safety pamphlet. Her mood began to lighten. The pictures made her smile. With all that she would have to conquer, she found relief in these funny stick figures falling off toilet seats. She read out loud the text printed in the pamphlet: "Share the know! Remember: Never lock your bathroom door! Safe and happy every day. Know how to: one, get on and off the toilet; two, get in and out of the tub. Know the bathroom hot spots! Know the hot spot solutions!" *Sounds painful.* "One in three people fall off the toilet . . ."

"Read the suggestions for the equipment to get," her mom said.

"A bath bench, a nonskid bathmat, an elevated toilet seat—oh, please no! Not *that.*"

Her mom stopped writing and looked at her. "No one's going to see you on it, Cat. Except me. And you'll probably not need one."

"I better not," Cat said.

Her mom returned to her list. "A night-light. I think we have one in the drawer in the bathroom. And I thought we should find the baby monitors we used for you and Buddy. You can place one on your nightstand, and I'll have one on mine. Then you can call for me anytime during the night."

"Good idea, hon," agreed her dad. He rinsed out his coffee cup and placed it in the sink.

"I'm not an infant," Cat whined. But she agreed to herself that it was a good idea.

Her dad pulled a chair beside her. "Cat, you'll need some extra care right now. It's a lot to get used to, I know, but one step at a time." He looked at her leg casts. "One goal at a time."

"Yeah, okay." She put her hands on the armrests. "Can you hand me another pamphlet?" He showed her the others, and she pulled the one with the dog on the front of it. "We could get an assistance dog for me, since Buddy will be away at college." Her brother was allergic to just about every animal. Then she thought about the money that would be needed to take care of a dog. *They're already spending a lot of money on me and Buddy.*

"We can think about that." Cat knew her mom was just appeasing her, but she understood.

Buddy shuffled back into the room. He was showered and dressed. Pouring himself a cup of coffee, he said, "Hey, Dad. Can I borrow your car?"

A moment later, Cat heard the motor running. The sound made her stomach hurt.

"Could someone pour me a glass of orange juice, please?" she asked.

"Sure, honey. Hey, you ate all your pancakes! Good job." Her dad picked up her plate, walked over to the sink, then got her the glass of juice.

Her mom placed the pen on the table and looked at her list. "I think that's a good start."

Cat's mind raced. So many things to consider. It all was too overwhelming to think about. Her dad was right: one thing at a time.

❧

In her bedroom, Cat sat in her wheelchair holding the football and looking out the window at the field. She sighed. *No more running, throwing, catching.* Still, she wanted to go outside. *I could go into the barn.* "Are you going out there to pout?" she could hear her mom say. As a child, she spent hours in the cavernous space playing with dolls and toy cars and trucks. When she started school, it was the best place to do her homework. Now, she craved the space to think. Stress again arose from her stomach to her chest and her mind. She wasn't prepared for so much change to come into her life.

And all of it *before* the accident. She'd been heartbroken at learning that Buddy would be moving to Florida for college, then her parents had announced that the barn would be turned into a studio apartment that would be rented. Losing her brother and her favorite place! She couldn't stop obsessing over what was being taken away from her.

After a couple of yells for her mom, her mom showed up and rolled Cat into the field, not too far from the house.

Cat put the wheelchair brakes on. She thought about her newest problem: the casts and chair. The casts did not bother her as much as she'd thought they would. They didn't itch like she'd heard they might. What was challenging for her to accept was being confined to the chair and being dependent on her family and friends to get around. *I've only been in this wheelchair for seven days. Breathe. Relax. I'll be okay. One, in and out, two, in and out, three, in and out, four, in and out, five, in and out. But I still feel stressed.*

The football rested in her lap. She was tempted to throw it up in the air but was afraid she couldn't catch it or, worse, that she'd fall out of the wheelchair. She'd felt claustrophobic inside the house and now felt stuck outside too. There was nothing to do in the field while she was in a wheelchair. And she no longer needed to practice for the Thanksgiving football game. *So much for being the quarterback. Or even playing!*

Behind her, she heard the front door open and close. Her mom was coming to bring her back into the house. *It's been twenty minutes? And I've just been sitting here.* She heard footsteps behind her.

"Ready to go back inside? Here we go," her mom said.

Here we go, Cat lamented. *What's next?*

❧

Ten days had passed since the accident. The car was totaled, so the family was left with only one car. Uncle Hal offered his truck, but Cat's parents figured they could manage with her dad's vehicle.

Cat practiced her means of transportation around the house. School would start next week, and she'd have to be able to get around the halls on her own or, more realistically, with the help of her best friends, Hattie and Gwilym, who were cousins. She couldn't help being frustrated. Managing on her own seemed impossible, especially with the leg extensions attached to the front of the wheelchair. Because of the extensions, she was unable to turn around in the hallways in the house. In the barn, it was no problem. *But that didn't matter now that some stranger was moving in there. I could have moved in there. It could have been my bedroom!* She teared up.

It was midmorning, and her brother had wheeled her into the kitchen, then he'd sat back down at the kitchen table to continue grazing through his college books. Their mom was peeling carrots for soup at the kitchen sink. Cat adjusted her seat to get more comfortable.

The room was quiet. She locked her wheels and folded her hands in her lap. She had forgotten to bring something to do. She was stuck here. *I can't ask Buddy to take me back into my bedroom. And he looks too engrossed in his textbooks to disturb him anyway.*

"Buddy, how do your course books look? Interesting?" asked their mom. Cat noticed that she looked tired. But she was smiling at Buddy. "I can't believe you're going away . . . my baby."

"Yeah, good," Buddy answered. "This"—he held up a book—"is *The Wound Dresser* by Walt Whitman. It looks like it will be a good read."

"So, do you think you might major in English literature?" She peeled another carrot.

"Yeah. Probably American literature—like Whitman. My sophomore year we read *Leaves of Grass.*"

"That's good," their mom said. Her head was bent down, making her voice less audible.

Cat noticed the side of her mom's face redden. She sniffled and wiped her nose, then put down the peeler.

"I'll be right back," she said quietly.

Cat saw the tears in her mom's eyes as she passed, heading down the hall.

"Mom's crying," Cat whispered to her brother.

"What?" He looked up from the book.

"Mom was . . ." Cat began. *Buddy can be so oblivious.* "Never mind." She placed her hands on the wheelchair locks. "Will you take me to the porch? I want to try Uncle Hal's ramp."

"Sure," he said.

She looked at his face. He was distracted. And she didn't blame him; he was starting a new life. Cat could take care of their mom, if she needed to. Maybe she was overreacting. But something was different in her mom's manner, in how she'd left the kitchen. *Why am I feeling upset? Is it my fault Mom is sad?*

With Buddy behind her, Cat rolled the wheels forward using all her strength. *How fast can I go down it?* The wheels gained speed, and it began to dawn on her that she might not be able to slow down. She breezed past Buddy down the wood ramp and screamed. *I'm going to be flung out of my wheelchair!*

But Buddy was there in time, swinging his muscular arm around her and hauling her back into the chair. "What were you thinking, Cat? Geez." He was breathing heavily, and sweat glistened on his forehead.

Cat looked at the end of the driveway and saw her best friend, Hattie, a familiar, short figure with shoulder-length black hair, race up the driveway to them. "What was *that,* Cat?" she asked. "That could've been bad!" She grabbed the handles of the wheelchair.

Buddy scolded his sister. "If you injure yourself again, you'll be in big trouble."

"I'm okay," Cat said, her heart pounding in her chest. *That was stupid. What was I doing? Was I trying to hurt myself?*

"Hattie, don't let her do anything else stupid," Buddy warned, retreating into the house.

"I won't, I promise. Where do you want to go, Cat? How about inside the barn?"

"To the barn," Cat said, stretching her arm like an arrow. She was calming down.

They remained a moment at the barn entrance. Cat scanned the white walls that covered the wood beams. She remembered how slivers of sunlight snuck through the vertical planks. To bring in light again, her dad, Uncle Hal, and Buddy had installed two skylights. These large openings to the sky kept the room warm and inviting.

It's still mine. It's still mine until he moves in.

"Wow. Looks completely different," said Hattie. "I remember running around in here when we were kids."

The entrance to the studio-barn was wide, making it easier for Cat's wheelchair to sail through. In this large space, it could turn around in a circle. And so her friend spun the chair about while they laughed. Cat relished this silliness.

"So . . . when is Buddy going to school?"

"August 19." Cat quickly changed the subject. "Let's look at the mural."

"I don't know that I've ever looked at it closely," Hattie commented. "Wow. The little figures are so cute. Your great-grandma painted this of the farm and Sourland Mountain, right?"

"My great-great-great-grandma Jewett—I don't know how many greats. We just refer to her as Great-Grandma Jewett. See the date down there on the right? It was painted in 1856. My mom told me it's in the style of the artist Grandma Moses. And look, there's Uncle Hal. My mom painted the picture of him when he moved into the original farmhouse three years ago."

Hattie took a few steps back to better examine the entire picture.

Cat rolled herself closer to the mural. "In the back is Sourland Mountain. And those hump-like shapes painted in light blues and greens are the Backwoods"—she paused—"where we crashed." She pointed to a blue undulating line that went between the mountains and the fields. "The fields are where the new houses are being built now. And in front of the picture is our family farm, or what used to be the running farm."

Hattie leaned over to inspect the small cows and horses. "You don't have farm animals."

"No animals, just Uncle Hal's veggie gardens."

Hattie looked elsewhere in the mural. "I like the galloping horses and the ones pulling the people in carriages." She then surveyed the room. "Your dad and uncle and brother did an amazing renovation in here. Everything looks great! This is a huge space for an artist to paint in." She looked at the stairs on the right that led to the apartment with a kitchen, living area, and bedroom. "Were you able to go up there before the accident?"

"Yes. Go check it out," Cat encouraged Hattie.

Hattie ran up the stairs. She took a quick look around and was back by her friend's side. "So, when is the artist moving in?"

Cat's stomach jerked, but she worked to hide her anxiety from Hattie. "He's moving in soon. His name is Benton Whitman. He's an old friend of Uncle Hal's from college. My uncle and parents went to an art gallery opening of his work."

"What's a gallery opening?"

"I think it's an event where you go see someone's art, and then you can buy it."

"Did your parents buy any?"

"No. They said it was too expensive. They couldn't afford it now! With paying for college, and now me." Cat gestured to herself. *I'll also have physical therapy later. Yikes.*

But Cat did feel less stress about these things with Hattie here.

It was almost dinnertime, so the girls decided to go into the house.

"Mm, what's for supper?" Hattie said. "Smells good."

"I don't know, but my dad's cooking, so something good."

The two girls headed for the kitchen.

"Thanks for moving me around today, Hat," said Cat.

"How else are you going to get around? It's kind of fun. Maybe I'll have big muscles by the time you get out of your casts." They giggled.

They moved into the kitchen, where they found Cat's dad pulling a dish from the oven, and an aroma filled their nostrils. "Meatloaf!" the two exclaimed.

"Hattie," Cat's dad said, "we're going to have to do something nice for you when my daughter's recovered. I can tell that you're going to be a big help to us."

Hattie's face reddened. "She'd do the same for me."

"Of course," Cat said.

Cat's mom was mixing a salad. Buddy was filling the water glasses around the table. Hattie placed the TV tray over her friend's legs.

"Next week you can take me to work, then you can have the car," said her dad.

"Okay," agreed her mom. *She doesn't sound very enthusiastic. Almost hesitant.*

Cat looked at her mom, at the circles under her eyes. She looked stressed. *But why?*

"Are we ready for this artist to move in?" her mom asked her dad.

"I think so. Last thing is Hal checking the plumbing again. Then it's ready."

Cat waited for the lock on the barn door to be mentioned, but no one spoke. They were all concentrating on eating. Except she noticed her mom's meatloaf remained untouched. *It's one of her favorites. Is something wrong with her?*

"The meatloaf's awesome as usual, Dad."

"Yeah, Mr. Hamilton. I love eating at your house."

"Aren't you hungry, Mom? Are you feeling okay?"

"I don't have much appetite, I guess. I'm fine, though." She shrugged.

Cat glanced at Hattie. She wondered if her friend noticed anything about her mom's behavior. But Hattie wore her usual happy expression.

Maybe it was better if Hattie didn't notice anything different about her mom. When they were together, they could be best friends hanging out. She wouldn't have to think about her mom.

❧

It was the evening before the artist named Benton was arriving. Cat rolled herself around inside the barn, contemplating this big change in her life—the loss of her favorite place. *Okay, I'm going to be calm and not worry about this stranger moving in here. It'll be all right.* She took five deep breaths, counting each one. *The last time I'll be able to be in here by myself . . .*

❧

It was morning, and Benton would be here soon. Cat decided she'd be the first to greet him. *Let's see if he's worthy of taking over my space.* Earlier, Cat's mom had been pulling weeds around the studio-barn entrance. It was hot outside, Cat noticed, as her mom had sweat on her cheeks when she stopped by to check on Cat. While she primped around the barn, the men had done a walk-through of the studio and apartment.

A green pickup truck with its back filled pulled onto the Hamiltons' gravel driveway. Cat listened to the tires grind over the surface as she watched the vehicle approach. She could see the man in it was wearing a hat, an old-fashioned one with a wide brim. He stopped his car beside the red barn *that was now his.* He parked and got out.

She squinted at the stranger as he approached. *I'm not going to be won over easily.*

"Hello," Benton said. His thick, wavy reddish-brown hair curled out from under the hat. He had a mustache and a beard with a white stripe on either side of the tips of his smile.

"Hello. I'm Catalynd." She shook his hand, as her parents had taught her to do.

"Cat-a-lynd. I like your name. My name is Benton." He looked at her leg casts.

"My mom and I were in a car accident. We crashed into a tree."

"I'm sorry," he said. Cat looked at Benton's face. She saw his eyes were gray, and they were calm and sincere, not intimidating.

A moment later, the rest of the Hamilton family was surrounding the new tenant.

"Well," said Benton, "I better start bringing in my boxes. The moving truck should be here any minute. They weren't far behind me."

"We can help," Cat's dad offered. Buddy nodded.

Everyone turned as a large truck with a familiar moving company logo on its side pulled in. Cat thought it looked like Benton owned a lot of things. He kept apologizing to the movers for the heavy books. He stood by Cat as they unloaded. "I have too many books," he told her. She smiled and thought of the small bookshelf in her room. Maybe when she was Benton's age she'd have as many books as he did.

❧

The following week, Cat wondered what Benton was up to in what was now his home. *I want to see what he's doing in there.* But of course, she couldn't get there by herself.

Cat called to her mom. "Can you come in here, please?"

"Yes, what is it, Cat?" Her eyes looked puffy. *She must not have slept well last night.*

"Can we visit Benton? Can we see what he's doing? If he's not busy?"

"Okay. As long as we're not bothering him."

They stopped at the threshold to the studio-barn and saw the artist washing his hands in the big sink on the back wall. He wore his broad-brimmed hat and a paint-smeared jacket. *That must be his paint smock.* Cat recalled the painting smock she wore in kindergarten.

The huge skylights were bringing sunlight into the center of the room. In the corners of the room, where the light didn't reach, were unpacked boxes. But not many, and it was clear that Benton had been working on emptying them. Above the boxes, he'd tacked up his drawings. *This must be what it looks like inside an artist's studio.* Cat looked back to the center of the room at his work space, where a large painting sat on an easel with a stool beside it next to a big wood table with paint tubes, brushes in cans, pencils, and a stack of small black notebooks on top of it.

"Hi, Benton. May we come in?" her mom asked. "If you're not too busy."

"Of course. I would enjoy some company. I was about to take a break."

"Wow, you've been working," said Cat. "May I see your painting?"

"Yes. I'm in the final stages. What do you think? Do you like it?" He stepped beside it as Cat and her mom moved up to it. "It's an evening scene," he continued. "'Keep your woods O Nature, and the quiet places . . . ,' to quote a famous American poet, Walt Whitman. The landscape's colors. Do they remind you of being outside at night?"

"Let me see." Cat looked at the painting. "I don't know anything about art."

Her mom stood behind the wheelchair. "Try, Cat. What do you see?"

"It takes a lot of looking and studying," Benton said. "But everyone has a gut reaction to a work of art. That's why I'd like to hear your thoughts.

You've heard people say 'I know what I like and I know what I don't like.'"

"Or," her mom said, "they say 'My kid could do that!'"

"Then," said Benton, "you hope they can look at it again and try to understand what the artist is trying to convey to the viewer."

Cat stared at the picture. "Well, first off, it does remind me of a fall night, with the dark oranges, reds, and browns."

"Good. Do the colors evoke any smells for you?"

"Smells?" Cat stared at the painting.

Benton sat by patiently. "This might sound strange, but I imagine the smell of the candles my mom lights around our house for the different seasons, like the fall."

"Like the candles I put all over our house," her mom added. Cat wondered what candle scents would relax her mom.

"I would smell apples and cinnamon and wood burning and leaves."

"That's what I'd say," her mom agreed.

"And sounds?" Benton asked them.

"Owls," Cat said. Her mom nodded.

"I haven't put any animals in my paintings. Maybe I should."

"I like that idea," Cat said. "It could be like a game to find different animals in your pictures."

"That might be an idea," the artist said.

Cat looked around the barn that was now Benton's place. "This is your office, isn't it? Like my dad's office. Only his is nothing like yours. Yours is a million times better than his. My dad's room has plain white walls and a dark wood desk and bookshelves. He has pictures of us in it. There must be a framed picture on his wall, but I don't remember of what. A landscape? Building? I have no idea. Something boring. He should buy one of your paintings."

Benton smiled and picked up a paintbrush.

"Are they expensive? How much are they?"

"They start at two thousand dollars." He smiled a little sheepishly.

"I didn't mean to be too bold."

"That is quite all right. I will answer any questions you have about art."

"Cool."

"We appreciate your time, Benton. I hope we really didn't disturb you," said her mom, beginning to wheel her daughter out of the artist's studio.

"I should finish unpacking." He put the brush back on the enormous table.

Cat felt a warmth in her belly. *He's not too bad. I may not mind him being here.*

❧

It was the morning of the first day of school and Cat was in bed. When she awoke, she'd realized that the typical Hamilton family morning routine would be different from now on. Buddy was sleeping instead of racing around trying to find his schoolbooks and football equipment, which he always left all over the house. *Soon he'll be in his dorm room and bothering his roommate with his morning habits.* Cat preferred him being here and bothering the family. Her dad was at his regular station in the hallway, finishing pressing his dress shirt.

She hadn't heard her mom moving around. Her mom had said that she would help Cat get dressed.

At least she could do her own hair, since it was just a single braid.

"Dad?" He walked by. "Is Mom up? I need help getting ready."

"I'll check." She heard her dad go into the bedroom, then he returned to her door. "She's getting up." Cat was a fast dresser and always the first one at the door ready to go. No one ever had to wait for her. Now she had to wait for someone to get her ready. On someone else's schedule.

Her mom was usually up and cheery on the first day of school—talking about how it was a new year and new beginnings. But this morning when she came into Cat's bedroom, she looked like she'd barely been able to get out of bed. Together they got her dressed without a problem. "That wasn't too hard," said Cat. "Thanks, Mom." Her mom kissed her forehead.

"Cat, are you ready?" her dad said twenty minutes later. He stepped into the hallway that led to the front door. "Oh, good. You're at the front door." He wore a light blue button-down long-sleeved shirt and khaki pants. His gray hair was combed into place. When he returned home tonight, it'd be back to its natural unkempt look.

With her mom's assistance, Cat got herself and her casts into the back seat, and her dad put the wheelchair in the back of the SUV. She liked riding with her dad. He listened to jazz music, which was soothing in the early morning. She could have a chance to talk with her dad about her mom's appearance and behavior. But she didn't . . . she could only handle thinking about getting around school today.

They parked in front of the school building, and Cat felt special when her dad helped her out and the kids stopped to look at her wheelchair. For the first time since the accident, she felt that she was getting attention that she liked.

❧

It was Saturday. Cat and her dad were eating sandwiches for lunch in the kitchen. He made excellent sandwiches.

Cat looked at him and put down her sandwich. "Dad?" She followed his gaze out the window to where her mom was pulling weeds from the flower bed.

"Huh?" He looked down at his plate and picked up some potato chips.

"Do you think Mom is okay?" She moved some chips around her plate.

"What do you mean?" He didn't seem affected by her question.

They both stared out the window. Her mom wasn't there anymore. She'd probably gone to weed around the studio-barn.

"Well," Cat explained, "since the car accident, I've noticed she gets upset easily. She seems sad a lot of the time, and she often looks tired." It seemed to Cat that she was having to wait a century for her dad to respond to her question. He continued chewing the potato chips and seemed to be concentrating on the tabletop. "Dad? Did you hear me?"

"I did," he said in a harsh tone. "And you shouldn't talk about your mom that way."

Cat felt hurt. He rarely talked to her or Buddy like this. It was like he was reprimanding her. It was the way he talked when he was laying out a punishment for her or her brother.

Did I say something wrong? I just want to know that I'm not the only one seeing Mom act differently.

She tried again to explain. “I think that she sleeps during the day. When Hattie’s mom drops me at home, Mom looks like she’s been sleeping. The blinds are always down in the bedroom. She doesn’t make the bed in the morning. Ever since the car—”

“Cat, that’s enough about your mom. I said she’s fine. There is nothing wrong with her.”

“But, Dad, I just want to make sure that—”

“I’m not going to talk about it with you. Your mom is fine.” He looked agitated, but his voice broke with uncertainty.

Crushed and wanting to run into her bedroom to cry, Cat finally dropped the subject.

“Done?” he asked, taking her plate and glass off the TV tray and rinsing them in the sink. He came over to her. He paused, and she thought he’d kissed the top of her head like he usually did. But he just said, “Where do you want to go?”

“In my room, please. Thanks.”

He wheeled her down the hall and into her bedroom. Together they got her onto the bed with some reading material on her lap. He closed the door behind him. *That was unnecessary. He’s treating me like I’m being punished.*

Cat's insides flattened. Her dad had rejected her concern about her mom. *Why would he do that? I'm thirteen—old enough to understand when someone is hurting, especially someone in my family!* Things were only going to get worse. Tomorrow Buddy was leaving.

❧

Cat opened her eyes, then shut them. The first sunlight of the day came through her window without apologies. It was the morning that Buddy and her parents would be leaving for Tallahassee. They would move him into his dorm room, get him settled in, then they would drive back. They'd be away one full week. She could hear her parents and Buddy chatting excitedly in his bedroom. *Even Mom sounds upbeat. Maybe Dad is right. Maybe nothing is wrong with Mom. I still wish Buddy wasn't moving away. I may need him for support. Talking on the phone is not the same as him being here.* She felt alone, even with her family in the next room.

"Your grandma's here," said her mom. Cat's grandma would be staying at the house for a week. She liked when her grandma, her mom's mom, visited. She set up activities for them to do, so Cat was not bored during her visits.

Cat had asked to be positioned in the hallway, her wheelchair facing toward the front door. Her grandma wiped her feet on the rug. "Well, dear," she said, "you *are* getting around."

"Yes," she responded, rolling her wheelchair back and forth.

"I've got here in my purse a list of things for us to do while I'm here." Her hair was curly, gray, and short, and she wore her usual outfit: jeans, an L.L.Bean shirt, and walking shoes. Her grandma seemed to be always in motion and walked five miles every day. "I think first we should get out of the way. Shall I push you into the family room?" Her grandma backed her up and swung her around and into the room. "Whoa!" said Cat. "You've got muscles, Grandma!"

"Where do you want to sit?"

"Beside the couch." She could watch Buddy, her parents, and Uncle Hal parade down the hall with boxes that they were putting in the Range Rover. She would have been right there helping out, if she could have. The family always worked well together to get things done.

"We can watch them from here," her grandma commented.

"You don't have to sit with me, Grandma. I'm not going anywhere." She knew her grandma was not a fan of sitting around.

"No, that's okay. We can talk while they work." Her grandma crossed her legs and put her hands on her knee. "So, how's school?"

"Good." She watched Buddy walk by with a big box, then her uncle followed, and her dad. She heard her mom say, "Is that all of the boxes?"

"What are you doing in school?" her grandma continued.

"We have to do a report on an artist. Our teacher is requiring us to go to the library and take out four or five art books."

"Well, that sounds interesting." She uncrossed her legs and stood up. "I think they might be ready to go. Why don't we go outside?"

Cat's heart beat faster. She'd run through this moment in her mind many times.

Her grandma rolled her out to the vehicle. Her dad shut the trunk door. Beside him, her mom stood next to Uncle Hal.

Buddy came over to her. "I guess this is it. Wish you could come with us. Once you're out of those casts, you can visit the campus and my dorm room." He hugged her. When Buddy backed away, she saw tears in his eyes. "Well, all right, then, take care of yourself, kid." He punched her shoulder like he did after they threw the football. Benton came out from the studio-barn to shake Buddy's hand.

Cat, Benton, Uncle Hal, and her grandma waved as the car rolled down the driveway. Her grandma put her hand on Cat's shoulder. "We can go inside now, if you want." Cat nodded. "We'll stay busy today. There's a *Gilmore Girls* marathon on all day. But first, we'll need to check our list."

"Sounds good," said Cat. She felt reassured, now that it was just the two of them. She would be distracted by the activities her grandma planned for them. And there was the *Gilmore Girls* to watch. Watching the show together was their thing.

Back inside, at the kitchen table, her grandma consulted the list. "Your mom suggested you have homework to do. We'll have lunch, then I thought we could go for a walk, or I could take you for a walk." She winked at her.

Again, Cat didn't mind her grandma taking hold of the day—of the week—until her parents returned. Each day with Grandma was pretty much the same, and Cat liked the regimen.

Her class assignments weren't too bad, and she finished in time for lunch. Her grandma made them macaroni and cheese. *Yum.* They ate it in the family room while her grandma watched one of the news channels.

"What about lying down and resting? Your mom said your doctor encouraged you to take naps." Her grandma was playing the part of a babysitter. "I think I'm going to take one. Then we'll take a walk."

On schedule, after their rest, they rolled down Cat's street and onto the dirt road that led them alongside the Sourland Preserve. It was the route she and her mom had taken when the accident happened. Cat thought about her mom. How was she feeling in the car right now? She wondered how the trip was going so far and where her family was on the way to Florida.

"Grandma, do you notice anything different about Mom?" Her grandma pushed the wheelchair over the bumpy road, bouncing Cat. Like with her dad, there was no reply.

A cow appeared in the road ahead of them. "Do you remember when you and Buddy were little and we came upon a cow? Buddy was trying to act like he wasn't scared by the animal. Do you remember? Maybe you were too young. I was probably pushing you in a stroller because I remember now that Buddy was pretty young. Anyway, he wouldn't budge, and he was trying his hardest not to cry. So I had to hold him and push you in the stroller to get around the cow." *So I'm being pushed around like when Buddy and I were little, only now he's not here. What does this have to do with my mom?* The cow mooed as they passed.

She squeezed the armrests, tightening her grip. *Is Grandma mad at me or disappointed in me? Is she embarrassed to admit anything could be wrong with my mom? She's acting like Dad. I am not giving up until I get someone in my family to hear me.* "Grandma—"

"I heard you the first time," she replied with irritation in her voice. "Your mom is a sensitive person. She's always been like that. Your uncle always tried to take care of her when she was sad.

It's just something she had to grow out of. So, I do think the car accident has made her sad. I'm sure she's upset to see you like this."

Cat was surprised to hear her grandma speak so casually about her mom's behavior and wondered if she would say more. Her grandma took in a big breath, released it, then said, closing the topic, "Your mom is in a funk. I wouldn't worry about her. I'd leave her alone."

Cat's stomach lurched. Anger filled her mind, and tears filled her eyes. She said as calmly as she could, "Can we turn around now, Grandma?"

"Yes, my dear. And we should get in some of the *Gilmore Girls* marathon before they get back." Her voice sounded normal again.

Cat was dismayed by her grandma's dismissal of her mom's condition. *Doesn't anyone care? Or am I overreacting? Am I being too sensitive?* A wave of fear flowed through her. *Am I going to be like Mom? And will no one care about me?*

The last night of her grandma's visit arrived. She and Cat were watching the end of a *Gilmore Girls* episode when bright car lights streamed through the family room. A moment later, her parents were standing in front of them, looking exhausted.

"Well, how was the trip? I made some dinner for you," said her grandma. Her parents followed her into the kitchen. They said the drive was no problem, and Buddy's dorm room was a typical, basic room, and the campus was not too large. They didn't have much to say.

Uncle Hal came in to check on his sister and brother-in-law too.

After everyone was finished with the meal, Uncle Hal volunteered to clean the dishes, and Cat said she'd help dry them. If they were alone in the kitchen, she could ask him his opinion about her mom. He was her last hope.

"Uncle Hal?"

"Yes, champ?" He handed her a plate.

Cat dried it and placed it on the counter. "Do you think something's different about my mom?" She was prepared for any reply at this point.

"Yes." He rinsed out a glass. "I do. She looks tired . . . When your mom and I were young, she was sad sometimes, maybe you could say depressed. When she was like that, I would try to comfort her."

His response was what she had waited for from a family member, but she was surprised by her reaction. It only worried her more. *That doesn't help me figure out how to help her.*

"She will get better, I promise, Cat. She'll be okay." He handed her another clean dish.

Cat grinned at her uncle. He was a kind man. But once again . . . maybe Buddy . . . but her gut told her that he was too busy with college, and he wasn't here anymore to observe their mom.

After school the following week, Cat, Hattie, and Gwilym moved through the automated doors of the Sourland Mountain library into a well-lit entryway. The girl at the reference desk could have been Buddy's age. Her thick, dark hair was wrapped up on top of her head, and the frames of her glasses were bright cherry colored. She told them what floor contained the art books. They moved past the library staffer to the elevators. This building was two years old. The walls, doors, and floors were sparkly.

"Cat, let's look first at the *Nancy Drew Diaries* series to see if they got any new ones in."

Gwilym followed his cousin and his friend over to the shelves where the Nancy Drew books were. "I guess the new one isn't out yet," Hattie said, disappointed.

The friends then waited at the elevator. Luckily it was empty, because with the leg extensions on Cat's wheelchair, she took up the entire space. The doors opened again, and they moved into a large room with a high ceiling.

"Wow," Cat said. "They really made this place big."

"Our art report is due in October," Hattie read from the assignment sheet. "October 24 . . . right before Halloween . . ." She looked at her friend's two leg casts. "Are you going to be able to go trick-or-treating with us?"

"I don't know. I don't even feel like thinking about my costume."

"And you usually have it planned by now," said Gwilym, nudging Cat's shoulder.

Hattie returned to reading from the assignment sheet. "Write about an artist. You will give a presentation on the artist."

"I don't know why we have to start so early on this report," complained Gwilym. The girls ignored him.

"Who am I going to write about?" said Cat.

"Artists? I can't think of any," Hattie mumbled. "I like pictures of cats and dogs."

"Dogs and cats and flowers. That's a good start," Cat said.

"If you're giving an art report on calendars," Gwilym remarked.

They went down the rows. Hattie sat on the carpet and pulled out books. "In these pictures, they're wearing old-fashioned clothes. These are old, old paintings. I don't think I like them. The people look funny. And so do the animals." She put that book down and leafed through another. She turned a page to a picture of *Starry Night* by Vincent van Gogh. "I like this one. My mom has a calendar of his paintings in her office." She looked up at Gwilym and smiled. "I'm going to write about him and this painting."

"That was quick," the boy said. He was flipping through book after book.

Cat had put a stack on her lap and couldn't find a painting she liked. The book on the bottom was *Andrew Wyeth: People and Places.* She stopped at an image of a girl in a large field with a barn and house in the distance. She read to them:

"*Christina's World* was painted by Andrew Wyeth in 1948. It's tempera. Christina couldn't walk, but she wouldn't allow anyone to feel sorry for her or help her. She refused to use a wheelchair, and so it took enormous strength to pull herself from the house to her parents' graves, which she visited regularly . . . I've seen this painting before. I always liked it because it's mysterious. And it reminds me of our field."

"I think it's creepy," Hattie said. She had kept her book open to the van Gogh work.

"There would be a lot to talk about. Okay, Hat, have we decided on our artists?"

"Yeah. Now I need to find enough books that have Vincent van Gogh in them."

Cat selected *The Arts: A Visual Encyclopedia, Gardner's Art through the Ages: The Western Perspective, Janson's History of Art: The Western Tradition,* and *Andrew Wyeth: People and Places.* She opened the Gardner's book and flipped through it. An artist's name appeared before her: Thomas Hart Benton. *I wonder if Benton is named after this artist. Mom said his last name was Whitman. Is he related to both of them, a famous writer and an artist? He hasn't mentioned if he is. I haven't asked him. That would be cool if he were named after two important people in history.*

"All set?" Hattie asked them. "Everyone has the correct number of art books to take out?"

"Yes, I do," said Cat. "I'm ready to go." She looked at Gwilym, who was holding four books, two with the name Paul Cézanne on the spines.

❧

When she arrived back home from the library, Cat was tired. After a nap, she decided she wanted to sit near the barn while her mom planted yellow flowers along the edge of the building. They looked pretty against the red barn. She studied her mom. *Should I just go with my family's advice and leave her alone? I don't want to bother her. I don't want to embarrass her or make her feel worse.*

But then Cat's dilemma appeared to be resolved when her mom lamented, "Oh, Cat, I used to love gardening." She sighed, looking at her daughter with a sad expression. "But now I find it laborious and tiring." Her shoulders slumped as she brushed soil off her knees and legs.

"What do you want to do?" Cat asked. "How can I help you, Mom? Can I do more chores? Can I clean for you?"

They were next to the barn entrance. "Does the house look that messy? I guess it does look a bit untidy . . . Your dad hasn't said anything . . ." *That's not a surprise. Of course he hasn't!*

Her mom sighed. "I'll get it together. Anyhow, it's nice to see that you two have become friends. You were sure he would be a terrible person." She hugged her girl. "And thanks for being concerned about me." She went back to the house. Cat would text her when she was ready to go in.

"Hi," Cat called to Benton, who was at the back sink. "It's your little pest coming to invade your space again."

"You are not a pest. And I understand from your uncle that this was *your* barn until I invaded it. So I certainly cannot banish you from what was originally your castle." *My castle. I like that. My castle barn.*

On the way into Benton's studio, she saw that the barn door latch still had not been repaired. Benton was probably too polite to mention it, or he felt safe enough without a lock on his place. But for Cat, the significance of the broken lock was that her mom had seemed to have forgotten about it, which was not like her usually observant and organized mom. If Cat's mom were her normal self, she would not have missed it.

She had brought the books about Thomas Hart Benton from the library. Cat propped the top art book on her lap. "These books are from the Sourland Mountain Public Library. I wanted to ask you something about one of the artists. I'm not doing my report about him, but he has a name that I wondered if—"

"Oh, so I see. What did you want to ask me?" he said with a smile.

She handed the book to him, and he glanced through it. "Are you named after Thomas Hart Benton?"

"I wondered whether the library would have a book on him," commented Benton. "And yes, I was named after Thomas Hart Benton."

"One mystery solved about our resident artist."

"What's the other mystery?" He raised his eyebrows in anticipation.

"First, tell me about Thomas Hart Benton. Please?"

"First off, Thomas Hart Benton was my mother's favorite artist, so that's why she named me Benton. Thomas Hart Benton was a famous American artist. His style is very recognizable with its swirling figures and landscapes. Here is a picture of his *Cradling Wheat.* It's one of my favorites. It's often in my mind when I'm drawing in a rural area like this one."

"Why do you like it?" Cat asked.

"It's a rural scene . . . a rhythmic scene. You could look up Grant Wood too. It demonstrates his passion for hard work. And can you see? Everything's dancing. Because of the lines he makes. The workers, the wheat, the trees, the hills, the clouds, the air. The scene could be on a stage. It could be a set for a musical on Broadway. Every line Benton made creates a highly dramatic movement. Can you see that? Nothing is relaxed, stable. All of life in this painting is in constant vibration. His mind must have felt a constant twanging. His strokes are very musical. I think it'd be easy to compose a tune for this painting."

Benton, having completed his thoughts, handed her back the book and picked up a paint-brush, cocking his head at his painting.

Cat was dazed by his words. "I suppose that kind of information will sink into my brain eventually. So, where were you born?"

He held his paintbrush in front of his painting. "In Pennsylvania."

"Have you lived in other places?"

"I've lived in a couple of places." He laid down his brush and sat on the wooden stool by his easel to give her his full attention.

"Where?" She was glad he wasn't annoyed about being interrupted.

He tapped his finger on his beard. "Oh, let's see. Besides Pennsylvania, New York, D.C., New Orleans, and now New Jersey."

"That's a lot of places. I've only lived here. How long have you lived in New Jersey?"

"Two years. A friend of mine lives in Princeton. He suggested that I relocate here. Some of the best art galleries are in Princeton, he said. I looked at art galleries, then for a studio."

"Have you always been an artist?"

"Yes. I guess I have." Benton considered. "I lived in Virginia too, forgot that." He nodded his head. "I taught art there."

"I think my mom is good at art." She looked at Great-Grandma Jewett's mural.

Benton followed her gaze. "That looks very similar to a Grandma Moses painting."

"That's what I've heard," said Cat. She thought about her family history and felt compelled to ask him about . . . what, though? How could she ask him about depression? It wasn't something you discussed. She was getting to know Benton. Could she ask him what he knew? Maybe first she'd explore the other mystery about him. "Benton?"

"Yes?" He continued applying broad brushstrokes across his painting.

"Are you related to Walt Whitman?"

"Yes, I am."

"Wow, so you're related to a famous writer and named after a famous artist. My middle name is Jewett. I like that I'm named after my grandma who painted that."

"That is special," Benton agreed.

"I have something to ask you. I mean, I wouldn't generally ask someone about this because I don't know you that well, and it's kind of a . . . It's just that I have no one to talk to about it, and you seem like you—"

"What do you want to ask me, Cat?"

"My mom has acted different since the accident." She thought of all the ways her mom had changed.

"How?" He moved the stool closer to her.

"Like being sad a lot of the time, not caring about her appearance, seeming too tired, and sleeping more than normal. I don't know what to do. My dad and grandma, even my uncle act like it's not a big deal. They tell me that my mom will get over it. But I don't know. She said today that she doesn't like gardening anymore. That's really not like her." Cat braced herself for another adult to tell her to stop worrying about her mom.

"Maybe the car accident triggered something in your mom," Benton said. "A traumatic event like what you both experienced could bring about those changes in her mind . . . But I don't know. I only just met your mom. So, unfortunately, I'm probably not helping you either. Walt Whitman dealt with depression in his life. Yet he was still able to write incredible prose and poetry. So depression is in my family . . . maybe it's in your family too."

Cat wondered if Benton had depression, but she wasn't going to be so bold as to ask him.

He continued, "Depression is common, but society still finds it hard to talk about, especially if it's in your family. That may not make you feel any better about what your mom is going through. But it is treatable. Many people with depression see therapists and are on good medications so that they can live normal, productive lives."

This talk was helping Cat feel better about the situation. "Thanks, Benton. You've made me feel hopeful that things will turn out okay. I suppose I should go now and do my homework."

Cat pulled her phone from her pocket and texted her mom. *I do feel better.*

"Cat," Benton asked, "would you like me to teach you some things about art?"

"Yeah!" Her eyes widened with enthusiasm. "That'd be cool."

"Great," said Benton. "But ask your parents first if it's okay."

SEPTEMBER

Through the ample open door of the peaceful country barn,
A sunlit pasture field with cattle and horses feeding,
And haze and vista, and the far horizon fading away.

—*A Farm Picture* by Walt Whitman

Benton had thumbtacked this poem next to the mural. Cat nodded to herself in agreement: Whitman's words suited the mural. Benton had lived in the studio for a month, and today they were just hanging out, talking about things other than art.

But now Cat could tell that her friend was eager to share something. He had a book in his hand. "I noticed your brother had this in one of his boxes for college. It's called *The Wound Dresser.* It contains letters written by Walt Whitman during the American Civil War. Whitman visited wounded soldiers in the army hospitals in Washington, DC, then he wrote accounts of what he saw and descriptions about how he helped the young soldiers through their illnesses and surgeries by doing little things for them, like bringing them fruit or paper and pencils to write a letter to their loved ones. I thought maybe you'd like to hear some of his letters, since Buddy will be reading them too."

"Yes," Cat replied. "Please."

Benton sat on his stool and began reading: "So this is what Walt Whitman wrote in his journal. He documented what he saw in the hospitals where he volunteered during the war. Entry one: 'Began my visits (December 21, 1862) among the camp hospitals in the Army of the Potomac . . . I had nothing to give at that visit, but wrote a few letters to folks home, mothers, &c. Also talked to three or four who seemed most susceptible to it, and needing it . . . I do not see that I can do any good, but I cannot leave them.'"

For Cat, listening to Benton read Whitman's words that he had written so long ago brought a calmness to the room. And the idea that Buddy might be reading the same words comforted her. It was like soft rain tapping on the studio-barn roof. Even though some of the letters were sad, she thought they were beautiful.

❧

Bearing the bandages, water and sponge,
Straight and swift to my wounded I go . . .
To each and all one after another I draw
near, not one do I miss . . .

—excerpt from *The Wound-Dresser* by Walt Whitman

❧

Beat! beat! drums!—blow! bugles! blow!
Through the windows—through the
doors—burst like a ruthless force . . .

—excerpt from *Beat! Beat! Drums!* by Walt Whitman

Uncle Hal came over that day to deliver a crate of his organic vegetables. He was standing with Cat and her mom. He was promising his sister that he would fix the broken latch on the studio-barn door today and giving them a weather report. "You have clear skies overhead, so *no* clever maneuvers with the car this time. Okay?" He put his hand on his sister's shoulder. She agreed. Cat and her mom planned to buy art supplies from the hardware store, since Cat was now interested in learning how to draw and paint. Her mom had finally asked for the car. Cat imagined that this was a big step for her. It was their first venture out since the crash.

❧

She started the engine, then sat and stared at the steering wheel and took a deep breath. From the back seat, Cat watched the keychain dangle from the ignition.

Her mom didn't say anything, just drew her hair behind her ears, then rubbed her forehead. She turned off the engine, her shoulders slumped.

"Are you okay, Mom?" Cat was able to reach her mom's shoulder. She placed her hand on it and felt her mom take a deep breath again. "I'm stuck back here, so I don't know what I can do to help you, Mom."

Cat's mom patted Cat's hand. "Thanks, honey. No, you can't do anything for me. I don't feel well. I just . . . I just don't think . . . I don't feel I can do it today."

Cat was confused. "I don't understand. Are you saying you're sick, Mom? Are you going to throw up?"

The keys were out of the ignition and resting in her mom's cupped hands. She was staring at them, and from the side, Cat saw a miserable and panicky look on her mom's face.

I don't know what to do. No one else is here, and I couldn't go get anyone anyway.

"Catalynd, I don't feel that I can. I feel like I can't make it today. I'm sorry." She returned the keys to her purse and opened the car door. Then she came around to Cat's side to begin the process of getting her out of the vehicle and back into the wheelchair.

Cat's head pounded. *What is wrong with her? Isn't there anybody to help me? To help us? I'm not responsible for her. I'm the only one who knows something is wrong with her, but I don't know what. I don't understand what is going on or how to fix her.* She felt alone.

Her mom held the wheelchair for her. Cat dragged herself into it again, refusing to look at her mom's face. Sniffling and creasing her forehead, she felt tired of her mom's behavior. *This is too much for me to deal with. Please, Mom, can't you just go back to your old self?*

Back inside, Cat was in the family room in front of the TV. She felt let down by her mom. Frustration set in, along with anger. She wanted to slam her bedroom door—maybe that would make her feel better. But instead, she felt terrible, like a completely selfish and mean kid.

She could hear her mom moving in her bedroom. She and her mom were the only ones in the house and the only ones aware of what had occurred in the car. Should Cat leave her alone, like her dad and brother were doing so far? *No.*

The easiest maneuver Cat could do in her wheelchair by herself was getting from the family room down the hall to the bedrooms. She rolled to the door of her mom's bedroom.

"Mom? May I come in?" She heard a quiet "Yes, dear." Automatically, her mom got up and worked to move her daughter into the room and then onto the bed. She got on the bed next to Cat. They sat with their heads resting against pillows and their legs stretched out in front of them.

The bed was comfortable. They sat for a while in silence. Cat compared her cast legs to her mom's legs and thought, *I need to remember what it was like having these lime-green casts on and what they looked like.* It was a rare light thought for her. Before long she ventured to ask, "Why couldn't you go out just now?"

"I feel like I can't. I feel so bad. Just awful." She hugged her knees. "I didn't expect to feel this way."

Cat stayed quiet. She was cooling down from being upset.

"I don't understand what's happening to me. Why I'm reacting to normal things the way I am. Like being in a car scares me. That doesn't make sense. Everyday things are harder for me to do. Even thinking about them makes me nervous . . . When do you feel nervous, Cat? When do you feel anxious?"

"I feel nervous in class sometimes. My stomach hurts when I have to get up in front of the class. Like when I'll have to give my art report."

"And when it's the day you have to give your report, and you're in your seat waiting, and you're next up, how do you feel?" She was beginning to look more relaxed. The blinds were down but the sun was shining, giving the room a soft glow.

"I feel like . . . I won't remember anything, or I won't be able to read when I get up in front of the class. That's what I think sometimes. That I'll forget how to read or talk."

"Do you ever feel trapped in a situation? Other than now."

Cat thought. She couldn't think of a time she felt trapped. "I don't think so."

"I remember giving a report at school," her mom said, "then feeling excited that I'd done it."

Cat didn't know what to say next. She didn't understand what her mom was going through. She could only wish she knew what to do. "Can I do anything to help you?"

Cat's mom looked thoughtfully at her. "I don't think so. I feel comfortable now. Safe. But more and more I feel completely overwhelmed. It's a horrible feeling. I begin to panic. I must have had a panic attack in the car just now." Her mom's shoulders dropped, and her hands were in her lap. Even her familiar voice sounded different. It'd always been soothing.

She was trying to understand what was happening to her mom, but she was feeling helpless. "Mom, you don't have anything to worry about. We love you."

"I know. So why do I feel so awful? I'm sad. And I don't know why. I'm scared, and I can't figure out why. The only reason I can think of is because of what's happened to you."

Now Cat was anxious.

She watched her mom pull a tissue from the box on her bedside table and wipe away tears. Her mom's legs were crossed, and she had a pillow over them with her hands folded on top.

I am so ready to be able to cross my legs. She rubbed the casts covering her knees.

"I'm trying to understand for myself what I'm going through. When I was Buddy's age, I felt like this. This fear—this unknown fear of everyday activities. I just want to feel normal again."

"I wish I knew what to do to help you feel better. But I don't know how to."

Cat noticed the circles again under her mom's eyes. "Your grandpa tried to understand too. He was a very sympathetic man. Like your uncle. He recognized that I may have depression, though we didn't call it that . . . I'll be okay. Don't worry. I'm sorry I'm putting all of this on you."

But you won't! You're saying the same thing everyone else in this family is saying, and I'm not going for it. "Mom, there must be something you can do. Someone to talk to."

"I have thought about talking to a therapist."

"I think you should. Because I'm really worried about you! And I have enough to worry about with my own problems." *I didn't mean for all of that to come out!*

Her mom leaned over and hugged her daughter and kissed her cheek. "I'm thankful you are here for me. I am sorry I've caused you so much anxiety." Cat whispered it was okay.

Then she got out of bed and maneuvered Cat back to the family room. They searched for any semblance of art supplies that might be found in the desk there. They laughed as she pulled out a collection of their pencils: a St. Patrick's Day one with a plastic green shamrock on top that used to light up; one with a metallic stars-and-stripes pattern; a variety of fluorescent-colored ones; and a yellow No. 2 pencil stained with blue and black pen ink. None of these pencils could she imagine Benton having among his art supplies. The mom and daughter laughed at the sad assortment.

Cat also found a clear plastic container for the pencils, pens, and markers. It wasn't the end of the world. Her mom had much bigger problems than Cat's at the moment.

❧

Cat's first art lesson was about to begin. She was on time. Her mom helped her into the studio-barn.

Cat felt happy the moment she saw Benton. He was a sturdy figure, standing in front of an easel with a big canvas on it. She considered him a friend by now.

"Good morning," Benton greeted them. Her mom nodded and left the room.

She smiled and rolled toward the center of the room next to her teacher. "I don't know if I can do any of this. And I don't have art supplies with me today. But maybe next time . . ."

"Of course you can. I believe that everyone has an artist inside them that just has to be gently coaxed out," Benton said. He spotted the clear plastic case in her lap.

"And as for the art supplies, that's okay," he said. "Now, let me see what you've brought. These will work. I've got a board with paper clipped to it that I think you'll be able to use."

Cat placed the board on her stomach. Then she turned it sideways and rested it on the armrests and straightened her back. "This should work."

"When you go to the store, you can get a drawing pad that fits better." He walked over to the large wooden table that held his art supplies.

"Wow," said Cat. "Your art materials are cool!" She parked herself beside them and inhaled a strong smell of chemicals. "What's that smell?"

"You must be smelling turpentine." He picked up a bottle filled with a yellow liquid. "Also, there's the oil paint and linseed oil that have strong odors." He handed her a tube of oil paint from the pile on the table.

She rubbed her fingers over the plastic cap on the tube. "The top looks burned. It's melted and black. What did you do to it?"

"The top becomes hard to open when the paint dries," Benton explained, "so lighting a match and circling it around the top loosens it. Fire heats the paint and expands the top."

"Oh, cool. Some of these look really old." She handed the tube of paint back to him.

"Some of these supplies belonged to my mother. She was an amateur painter." He arranged a couple of colors next to his painting.

"And the brushes. May I see some of them?" He gave her three different types of paintbrushes that he'd pulled out of the glass jars. Cat smelled them and touched the bristles—some were stiff, and others were soft.

"These brushes are used for details, and these for big areas." He took them from her and laid them next to the tubes of paint, then picked up a thin wooden board with a hole in it, which he put his thumb into. "This is my palette, where I squeeze globs of paint, then mix certain colors together." He demonstrated. Cat thought it all looked so impressive.

Farthest from the materials he'd just showed her was a collection of pencils, white erasers, and small black notebooks. He handed one to her, along with a pencil. "For sketching."

"Thanks!" She opened it to the first page and wrote her name: Cat Hamilton.

He pulled over a stool and sat beside her wheelchair. "What should we begin with?"

"I don't know." Her heart pounded with excitement.

"I thought we'd begin by learning about composition. Then we can try sketching," Benton told her. "Does that sound good to you?"

"Good to me," Cat replied. Although she wondered if she could do it and was a little worried about disappointing him if she couldn't.

"Let's begin by looking at the mural. Do you need help getting over there?"

"No. This place is big enough for me to get around in." She put the board securely across her lap with the notebook on top and the pencil on the right side between her and the seat. "Here I go." She maneuvered herself, feeling like a pro, over to the painting on the wall.

Standing to the left of the mural, he said, "Now, let's look at this picture. What do your eyes see first?"

"I see the two giant pine trees first, in front of the red-and-white checkered house. Two more tall pine trees are on the side of the horse stables, and then there are four more behind the other part of the stable and behind the barn (which is the one we're in now). This is what I noticed first."

He motioned her to continue. "What else catches your attention?"

She stared at it but didn't know what to say next.

Benton helped her out. "What colors pop out at you?"

"The red, then the yellow."

"And do they make patterns? The placement of the colors?"

Cat took a moment to consider the image. "At the top of the picture is the color blue for the sky, and the mountaintop is blue too. Then the field of hay comes next, the line of trees, the red buildings; then the dirt where the people and horses and carriages are a similar color to the land with the harvest of hay."

"Excellent! A quick lesson in beginning a composition: the artist makes a wash across the canvas of each section of color, so on the top she would paint—"

"A light blue."

"Then there would be an area of . . . Keep going. And skip the buildings."

Cat was enjoying this exercise. "Below the blue would be an area of blue-green, then the yellow, then green again, then yellow, and some green at the bottom."

"Can you name the sections of the painting? How it is divided up?"

"Like the background?" Benton nodded. She continued. "Middle ground and foreground! I remembered!"

Benton clapped. "Now back to the things in the picture. Do their positions lead your eye around the painting? Start at the bottom."

"The horses drawing the carriages are going to the right. They are galloping from the left side of the picture to the right side. But look! There are two that are going the other way."

"And what do they do? As far as your eyes."

"They . . . well, they're going the other way. So, maybe they stop your eyes from going off the side of the picture?"

"Good. They bring your focus back into the picture. Then where do your eyes travel next?"

Cat concentrated on the picture. "The red of the buildings catches your eye. They're in the middle, so they . . . they kind of stabilize the picture?"

"You are good at this. I'm impressed, Cat."

They became silent, just looking at the mural.

This isn't easy, but I've gotten the answers right so far. The middle ground is where everything's happening. The trees bring your eyes up to the fields and mountains because they are pointed at their tops like arrows. The big pine trees are next to smaller ones that curve up to the field. The left side of the field next to the larger field tilts upward to the mountain. And the people are all together at the bottom, so they're kind of lost. I wonder why Great-Grandma Jewett didn't put little figures in the background?

"Does the artist do all of this deliberately?" Cat inquired. "I mean, is she actually able to plan every detail in the picture so it works?"

"The artist tries as hard as they can to make it all work together. But I've always thought that some elements in a painting just decide to go together on their own without the artist's knowledge or realization. So, again, composition is the way things are arranged in a picture. A composition cuts up the picture into sections. It moves your eye around so it doesn't just stay in the same spot on the painting."

"I didn't know that," Cat said. "I hadn't looked at the mural like that before."

"Now you can use that technique when you look at other paintings." He went over to a line of shelves her dad and uncle had built beside the mural. Benton had filled it with books. He pulled out the Andrew Wyeth book. "What painting did you say you selected for your school report?"

"Andrew Wyeth's *Christina's World*." She watched him leaf through the pages.

"Here it is." He got up and rested the book on the board on her wheelchair and said, "Let's look at this. Where do your eyes go?"

Cat sat up to get a better look at the image. *This one's easy.* "Christina is what you look at first. Her foot is pointed down to the left-hand corner of the painting. Then her left arm is placed in front of her, and if you run your finger up from her fingertips, you land on the house. Then the house is on that line at the top, and your eyes go to the left, to the barn."

"That's the horizon where the house and barn are. Wyeth, starting with his figure of Christina, moves the viewer's eye across the entire picture. And there are really only three things in the large painting. Very good, Cat. Once more you're catching on quickly."

Benton and Cat went over to the canvas and art table. "Now, let's do something completely different. Let's make lines."

"Okay," said Cat. She opened her notebook like Benton did.

"Are you in a comfortable position?" He sat on his stool.

"Yes, as much as I can be. Thanks for asking." She put her pencil to the paper.

"I would like you to practice making lines. Long lines. Short lines. Thick lines, thin lines. Squiggly lines. Let's do that for a while, until I say stop."

Cat liked the pencil he'd given her. It made deep, dark marks when she pressed hard onto the paper. It made light lines when she lightly moved it across the sheet. "This is cool."

Benton smiled and continued to sketch in his notebook.

This was fun. It helped her get away from her problems. Her only problem now was that the wheelchair hindered her comfort in drawing. She had to keep pulling herself up in her chair because the seat was vinyl and slippery and her butt kept sliding down. She wasn't surprised Christina didn't like being in a wheelchair. Cat was paralyzed in her casts like Christina. *I wonder if I can drag myself out of my wheelchair and onto the ground? I should try it. If nothing else, I need some air for my brain to relax from all the information that's been inserted into it.*

❧

Benton helped Cat outside the barn. She told him she'd text her mom when she was ready to go inside the house. She was feeling on top of the world and had forgotten that her mom and dad were on their walk now. The field was in front of her. *It's like the one in* Christina's World. Cat was amazed by the paralyzed Christina. *How she dragged herself all that way.* Cat moved her wheelchair farther into the middle of the field. *Where could I try to crawl?* There weren't any graves to go to or objects that were close. Only the line of trees and Uncle Hal's house and green market were at the end of the property. *I want to see what it's like to get somewhere without a wheelchair, without being able to walk.*

She moved her wheelchair over the grass and dirt farther away from the barn and her house. A cool breeze blew across her face as she reached down to lock her wheels. She unhooked one of the leg rests so that it bent in half, then she released the other one, and they both fell away to the sides of the wheelchair. Cat hadn't done that before. Her mom was the only one who had done that for her.

"Wow," Cat said. Her legs felt heavy when they hit the ground. They weren't being supported by the braces anymore. *It feels strange. Now, how do I get onto the ground? It's like jumping into a cold pool—you just have to push yourself off the ledge.* She scooted herself to the edge of the seat. She sat for a moment. *Cold water.* Then she tipped forward onto the ground.

"Ouch." The ground was hard and colder than she thought it would be. She wore a long jeans skirt and tights with red and blue stars on them. They'd been relieved when the tights had slid easily over her casts. Cat was also wearing her favorite red down slippers. But she wasn't sure now that this had been a good idea. *But here I am!*

Cat leaned on her side to mimic Christina's pose. She was turned toward her house. *I may be half the distance she was from her house. This doesn't look fun. But I'm going to try to drag myself across the field. Maybe I can put this in my art report!* She moved her arm forward and dragged her body, then the other one and repeated the motion. *One—two—three—four—Christina's legs couldn't be as heavy as mine. Five—six—seven—Ugh! I don't like this!*

Rolling onto her back, she saw the rain clouds above her. She heard the light tapping of rain on the barn roof before she felt the first droplets on her face. The rain began falling, and she feared getting drenched. Now she remembered that her parents were on their walk. *They must be coming home soon!*

The raindrops hit the top of her head and rolled down her back as she started using her hands and arms to pull herself toward the house. *I don't know if I could even get myself into the chair again if I reached it.* In her tired mind, the best decision seemed to be to crawl to the house. Its white frame was blurry through the raindrops on her lashes and in her eyes. There was dirt and grass on her hands, arms, and elbows. Her cute tights would be all stained now.

She was nearing the barn. *Benton's inside! Maybe he can hear me if I yell.* "Benton!" But Cat's scream was silenced by thunder. The loud crash scared her into tears. Then panic! *My casts! They're getting wet!* She shut her eyes and imagined being in bed with soft pillows and warm covers. *After taking a hot shower! Oh, the day I can take a hot shower . . .*

Then finally, she saw two figures walking up the driveway. "Mom! Dad!" They heard her and began running to their stranded daughter.

Her dad got to her first and picked her up. "I'm sorry, Dad," Cat moaned. "It was stupid to come out here. I didn't see the rain clouds." He lifted her into the wheelchair. Her mom walked beside them. The rain had lessened.

After a hot bath *(that was pretty soothing!)*, Cat, in extra-large pajamas and wrapped in a blanket, was stationed in front of the TV watching her favorite show. Her casts had not been too damaged in the rain. The house was quiet except for the voices of Lorelai and Rory Gilmore.

❧

> A spell of fine soft weather. I wander about a good deal . . . a soft transparent hazy, thin, blue moon-lace, hanging in the air.
>
> —*The White House by Moonlight* by Walt Whitman

"The worst part of being in this wheelchair and these casts is being in here," Cat said as her mom helped her in the bathroom. "You'll be glad too, I bet, when you don't have to take care of me."

"Especially rescuing you in the pouring rain when you've decided to pretend to be a paralyzed girl in the middle of the field. And you decide to go out there by yourself when your parents are not home. Don't do anything like that again until you're out of this wheelchair!"

They headed toward the front door.

"Sorry." Cat tightened her grip on the armrests as they went down the ramp. *I'm not going on the ground again.* "But I did yell to Benton."

"Benton's not responsible for you. We are."

Cat looked at her mom. She was scolding her, but she was in her normal mode. "You seem like yourself, Mom."

"You are perceptive. I am feeling more like myself. I don't feel the same as I did before the accident, but maybe things are going to be okay." She squatted in front of Cat. "I talked with your dad, and he agrees with me that it's a good idea for me to see a therapist. I found a psychiatrist in

Princeton. Would you come with me, Cat? You'd just stay in the waiting room."

"Of course I'll go with you, Mom." Relief filled her insides.

"It seemed like the right step to take to try to feel better so I can do the things I used to do and enjoy them again. But you listening to me was a big help."

She did see my concern. And maybe just being there for her was enough.

"Let me roll you out to Benton."

❧

Cat had the board with the drawing paper clipped to it and a pencil and was ready to begin drawing. It was the beginning of another art lesson. When she came into the studio, Benton was standing beside the work table with a satisfied grin. He had cleared a corner of it and placed there a large white cloth with a ceramic bowl on top filled with oranges, apples, and lemons. "This is a still life. I modeled this one after a Paul Cézanne still life. I'd like you to draw it with a pencil, then we'll move on to paint."

"Cool," said Cat.

After a few moments of drawing, she stopped and looked. The bowl and fruit were scrunched into the corner of her paper. "My drawing is all wrong."

Benton looked at her work. "That's okay. Let's try contour drawing."

On a blank piece of paper, he placed his pencil at the bottom left and began drawing the outline of the base of the bowl, then around the edge of the oranges, the apples, and the lemon. He continued with the side of the cloth, then finished where he'd started. He drew the whole thing without looking at the paper, creating the outline of the objects.

"Now you go into each object and fill in the details. And see also how I used the whole surface for the picture."

"How did you do that so well?" Cat got a clean sheet ready.

"By practicing. Put your pencil at any point on the paper that corresponds to a section of the picture, or you can start at one of the corners like I did. Then you make a single, unbroken line. You look at the still life and not at your paper. Try to feel the objects as your pencil draws them."

Cat positioned the pencil tip where Benton suggested. She made a curve for the side of the bowl, then humps for the tops of the oranges, apples, and lemon, then swung the pencil around and down to the bottom of the bowl, and lastly, the cloth. Her lines met back at the top of the page. Hesitantly, she moved her eyes from the still life to her paper. "Not too bad. At least I covered the paper."

"That is better. Now you go back in and put in the details." He shaded the tops of the fruit. "*Shading* gives the objects depth. In a drawing you can do this by making lines close together, called crosshatching. See how I'm making Xs close together? Or another way is to draw the lines one way, and then cross back over them in the opposite direction."

Cat made lines around the fruit and bowl using this type of shading.

"You're doing a great job." He smiled.

Cat relaxed and drew on another piece of paper. She made big swirls with big swings of her hand. She was completely engrossed in her work, completely concentrating on her picture.

❧

Cat called Buddy the next day. They had spoken a few times since he had moved to Tallahassee, but those had been brief chats, since he was very busy with his classes.

"So, what are you going to be for Halloween this year?" he teased. "Since you like to figure out your costume far ahead of time."

"I don't know yet." She was in the family room with the TV tray, on which she had her homework. "What can a person in a wheelchair go as?"

"I hadn't thought of that," Buddy admitted. "When I picture you, I don't see you with your leg casts and in a wheelchair."

I know, me neither.

"I'd go online. I'm sure you'll find plenty of suggestions for costumes."

Cat could hear talking in the background, most likely his roommate chattering on his phone.

"Yes, I will do that."

"You could go as a car . . . Or maybe you don't want to do that," said Buddy.

Cat had an inspiration. "I know what I could go as."

"What?" He muttered to someone in his room.

"I could go as a painting. Gwilym picked Paul Cézanne for his artist for our art report. I could be a still life, with a bedsheet wrapped around me and fruit on my lap. I'd have to make the fruit out of something—like a basketball could be an orange and the football I could cover with yellow paper for a lemon. What could I use for an apple? Another basketball, maybe? Apples are the same size as oranges, right? Is that why people say apples to oranges?"

"That sounds interesting, Cat. Hey, I've got to go. We'll talk soon."

He hung up, but Cat barely noticed as she had moved on to press Gwilym's name.

"Hey, Gwilym. I've got an idea for my Halloween costume."

He laughed. "Go on."

"I'm going as a Cézanne still life."

"I've been looking at, like, a *million* of them. That could be a good idea. What would it look like? How would you make it?"

She explained her concept for the costume.

"That'd be cool." He sounded more serious now. "And why are you telling *me* this?"

"Because you'd go as Cézanne—and you would wheel me around the neighborhood. We'd be dressed as a still life and its artist! Sounds awesome, right?"

His voice became contemplative. "If I wore one of those funny moustaches and found a hat like the one Benton wears, and maybe he'd let me borrow his palette and a paintbrush."

"And a smock. You'll need a painter's coat. Okay, talk later."

Cat was psyched. She had a Halloween costume planned out.

OCTOBER

Monday was here, and that meant her class would give their art reports today. Cat sat next to Hattie in their classroom. The teacher had moved Cat to the back of the room at her own desk by herself. Her best friend was sitting next to her now so she could take her to the front of the room when it was her turn. She and Cat exchanged nervous glances. They had not given their reports yet. They both got nervous speaking in front of the class, so they'd decided that they would concentrate on the other's face when they gave theirs.

"Thank you, Gwilym. Now, who's next? How about you, Cat? Hattie can go after you, since she has to come up here with you."

Thanks. Like that doesn't make me feel feeble. Or feel less nervous. Or less aware of my classmates staring at me as I'm rolled to the front of the classroom.

As Hattie brought Cat past their teacher, the woman smoothed her dress. It had a print of a blue sky with clouds on it. Cat imagined her sailing out the classroom window and into the sky.

Whenever Cat was about to talk in front of the class, she always had the fear that she'd suddenly have to run to the bathroom. And now she was trapped in the wheelchair. *Breathe. Breathe. You're going to be okay.* She knew she didn't really have to go. *Has anyone ever run out of a room in the middle of a speech? It must not be possible to leave while talking in front of a group of people. It's just not done. But maybe I'll be the first one in history.* With her notecards on her lap and stationed in front of the class, she motioned to the tech person to project the image of Andrew Wyeth's *Christina's World* on the screen.

Fifteen minutes passed by for her much quicker than it had when she had practiced the talk at home. Cat concluded the art report with "Andrew Wyeth's best-known work is probably

Christina's World. Christina was his neighbor. She had a degenerative disease, which meant that she had lost almost all of her ability to walk. She refused to use her wheelchair, so she would drag herself hundreds of steps to the site of her parents' graves; it took her a long time to do this . . . Wyeth depicts her dragging herself down the slope to the grave site, which the viewers can't see in this picture. Her house is on a hill there in the distance. Christina is looking at her house, and it looks like she's about to or has begun crawling back there, which would be quite tiring. But this is Christina's world. According to what I've read about the painting, she did not allow anyone to feel sorry for her or help her. She hated her wheelchair . . . As you can see, obviously, I'm still in mine. I don't hate my chair. It's fun rolling around in it. I mean, driving it around. It doesn't roll me around."

Her classmates laughed, and she looked at her teacher to see if time had run out, but she motioned for her to continue. Cat closed with a quote.

"Andrew Wyeth saw in Christina . . . her struggle to move, a tall, thin girl who once moved swiftly . . . [In this painting he] paid her his highest tribute."

She nodded, for that was all she had to say. The class clapped. Their applause sounded louder than the other students had received, she thought.

❧

Halloween night arrived. Cat, Gwilym, and Hattie went trick-or-treating. Hattie went as a brown bear. The Paul Cézanne still-life costumes turned out spectacularly. Gwilym looked like an artist, and Cat was comfy wrapped in a big white sheet. Her dad had found a small plastic sled the kids had used when they were little and spray-painted it silver. It became a bowl for the various-size balls, including the football lemon covered in papier-mâché. He had helped to make her costume even better than she'd imagined it. And most of the neighbors gave Cat extra candy. It was a Halloween she would always remember. *If only Buddy were here too.*

The next thing that would happen would be the family listening to a horror story. When Cat's mom and Uncle Hal were kids, their parents had begun the tradition of sitting around a bonfire with the radio on a station that played a program featuring scary stories. Radio stations didn't play these episodes anymore, but they were available on podcasts. This allowed the family to keep the tradition going. Cat's dad had hooked up his phone to a speaker to hear the old-time radio broadcast of an episode of a Halloween horror story.

The temperature went down, which was perfect for the fall bonfire. Hattie, Gwilym, Cat, her parents, and Benton gathered around the firepit in Adirondack chairs. Even Cat got to sit in one of these chairs, the one that included a footrest. The trick-or-treaters had their big bags of candy beside their seats, and they were out of their costumes.

Everyone gazed at the impressive fire that Cat's dad had made. The crackling of the fire and the sparks shooting out from it were mesmerizing. Cat concentrated on the pine cones piled in the pit that to her looked like little villages, with the orange flames consuming them being the lights inside the villagers' homes. *This is my favorite season by far.*

Cat was the keeper of the s'mores supplies and sticks. This had always been her designated job, and she was not going to forfeit it because of her current condition. "Who's ready for another marshmallow?" Her mom and Benton each grabbed one and slid it onto their sticks. Her dad waved off her offer. "Maybe later," Hattie said. Gwilym cooked Cat a fourth marshmallow.

"Are we ready for the horror story?" her mom asked. "Yes? Here we go." She hit play, and the music of the radio drama began.

Only the snapping of the fire voiced its opinion over the sound of the program announcer as he launched into his introduction.

"By the master of horror . . . And now we listen to the tale of *The Figure in the Moonlight* . . . The woman screamed in terror as the hand came over her mouth in the darkness . . ."

Cat squinted at her mom from across the fire, trying to read her expression. Cat decided that she looked relaxed. She even smiled at one point. But Cat remained nervous. She couldn't tell what her mom was thinking. *I can't read her mind.*

But then her mom curled up in her chair and hugged her arms. "I'm content tonight."

Cat realized again that the best thing she could do for her mom was to support her and love her. She couldn't do anything more. After all, she was a thirteen-year-old girl, not a psychiatrist.

When the story was over, the announcer came on again. "That was the terrifying tale of *The Figure in the Moonlight* . . . Until next time, pleasant . . . dreams?" Then the sound of a creaking door closed the program. Around the bonfire, Cat's family and friends clapped and cheered.

Cat said, "Good one."

"Yeah, good choice, Mrs. Hamilton," said Gwilym. You know how to pick 'em."

"Best one I've heard in a while," chimed in Cat's dad.

"I think I shall put a dramatic figure into one of my landscapes," said Benton.

"Interesting idea," said Cat's mom. She got up. "Well, anymore s'mores, anyone? If not, I'll take the supplies from you, Cat."

Benton got up. "Thank you, everyone, for letting me join in your family tradition."

"Wait until the Thanksgiving family football game!" said Cat. She forgot that she might not be able to play in it. She was still thinking about how much better her mom acted and looked.

NOVEMBER

Cat's mom turned off the car engine. They had sung their usual Juice Newton songs, which made Cat feel confident her mom was going to be okay. They were in the therapist's parking lot. Her mom did the regular routine of getting the wheelchair out of the trunk and around to Cat.

"Do you want me to hold your hand? Or—" Cat realized that it would be difficult to hold her mom's hand while in the wheelchair. Her mom got them to the front door and up the ramp, through the sliding doors into the lobby and waiting room of the 1970s-style building.

"Who are you seeing?" asked the receptionist with an uninterested glance at Cat's mom.

About ten minutes later, the door opened, and a tall woman stood in the doorway. "Ready, Mrs. Hamilton?" The therapist smiled at her mom, then the door closed behind them.

Cat was alone in the waiting room. She was positioned in a corner fit for a wheelchair. The waiting room had an odd smell. She noticed a plant in a corner on the floor that had stained that area. Viewing the stain, she surprised herself by bursting into tears. At first she figured it was sadness that had overtaken her mind, that she was upset that her mom had to see a therapist. But then Cat realized that she was feeling relief because her mom was here. It might mean that things were going to get better. She grabbed a tissue from a box and wiped her face and blew her nose.

The therapy session seemed to go quickly, and there was her mom, closing the door behind her.

"Ready?" Her mom was smiling at her. She didn't seem to notice Cat had been crying.

"How'd it go, Mom?" she asked. Cat hoped the session went well.

"At first I felt nervous. But she made me feel comfortable almost immediately. Thank you for coming with me. I really appreciate it."

"You're welcome." Cat left it at that. She didn't want to pry.

Her mom continued. "It was good. She suggested medication. I think it's a good idea. She also reassured me that my feelings are legitimate and real. And that my sadness is as much a part of me as my happiness. I thought that was just a comfort to hear." Her mom hit the big button with the wheelchair sign on it to open the doors. The two headed to the car.

Once they were settled in the car, her mom said, "Cat, there's just one thing I need to know. When you rolled yourself down the ramp that time and nearly injured yourself again . . . and then finding you crawling on the ground in the pouring rain . . . what were you doing? Were you trying to deal with what I was going through?"

"I probably was, at least the ramp incident. But I also wanted to know what it was like to be paralyzed like Christina."

"Buddy told me about the ramp episode the last time I spoke with him."

"Why did he tell you that?" *We usually don't tell on each other.*

"He said he was concerned about me. He wanted to make sure his mom was doing okay."

"I'm glad he asked you how you are," said Cat, playing with her braid. *So, all this time he did think she was acting differently too!* Grinning, she shook her head. *My brother is a good guy.*

"You two don't have to worry about me. I'll be okay. Because now I have help. And another thing the therapist suggested is that I do something outside of our house, like volunteering. So, I thought I'd volunteer at the Sourland Mountain Preserve. I thought of doing that when it opened years ago."

"That's a cool idea."

"We could visit the tree," her mom suggested.

"The tree?" Cat dropped her braid.

"The tree we hit in the accident. I'm curious to see if it's okay."

"Oh," said Cat. "It would be there by the roadside."

"Well, it's only an idea." They turned onto their driveway. "I'll be there anyway."

Buddy flew home two days before Thanksgiving. He and Cat were in the field. He had coaxed her into attempting to play with the football.

He lobbed the football up into the air and caught it, while Cat rolled herself into position to catch the football.

"Okay," said Buddy, "I'll stand close and toss the ball. Like this." He was about five feet from her. She caught it. *Yeah!*

"Now move back," she said.

He stepped back about ten feet and tossed it again. Cat missed it. But for a moment she felt normal. Buddy tossed the ball into her lap next, so she only had to put her hands around it.

He ran up and punched her on the shoulder—a normal interaction she had with her brother. "Awesome job, sis."

That evening Cat was in bed in the dark. *Could I play?* Her fingers were taking out her braid. *I've always played in the game. If I had an electric wheelchair. That'd be cool.* She closed her eyes. A moment later, she opened them. *Referee—I can be the referee!*

The weather was pure fall with full sunlight and a cool temperature. The Thanksgiving football game was about to start. This year Cat was not going to be the quarterback. Instead, she was declared the referee. And it was made official, and both teams cheered when she came out in her wheelchair wearing her uncle's black-and-white-striped rugby shirt, her mom proudly behind her.

The red team was Uncle Hal, Benton, and Gwilym. Team blue was her dad, Buddy, and Hattie. Each player had a corresponding red or blue cloth pinned to them with their number on it. Buddy made Hattie quarterback, which Cat huffed about until her mom convinced her that her best friend was warming up the position for Cat for next year.

"We got a girl quarterback!" her mom said enthusiastically. "And more importantly, *you* are the first ever *female* referee in a Hamilton family Thanksgiving football game!" Cat thought that was quite acceptable. *My best friend and I are breaking traditions!*

The game was tight. Both sides played well. And not many penalties.

On the final play, Cat blew her whistle. "Holding. Red. Number four. Yeah, that's you, Gwilym. Ten-yard penalty." The blue team won, and Gwilym protested the refereeing. Hattie gave Cat a high five. "I agree with your calls!" She laughed as she left to catch up with her cousin on their way back to their houses.

After the game, Cat's family and Benton were back inside the house. Her mom had lit the fall-scented candles, as she did every year. She blew them out before everyone sat down at the table to eat turkey, mashed potatoes, gravy, green beans, and marshmallows on top of baked sweet potatoes.

Cat's grandma sat in one of the high-back chairs. She'd call out the score of the game to whomever was in the room. She loved knitting and watching football. Out of the blue, she said, "It's been three years since your grandpa died, and I still miss him so much every day."

Watching her grandma knit, she was reminded of the stories about when she was a baby. Her grandma had been finishing up knitting a Christmas stocking like the one she'd knitted for Buddy. He was already called Buddy, not his real name, which was Benjamin. Unfortunately, her grandma spelled her new granddaughter's name "Catlyn." Cat could imagine hearing her grandma's question: "The baby's name is what? C-A-T-what?-L-Y-N? Say it again . . . Write it down . . ."

"How did your parents come up with your name?" Benton asked her while they sat on the couch watching the Dallas Cowboys and Washington Redskins. The Detroit Lions and Chicago Bears had already played the first traditional Thanksgiving Day game. Cat explained that she was named after her dad's parents, who had both died before she'd been born. Her dad's mom's name had been Catherine, so they took Cat from that; her grandpa's name was Lyndon, so they took Lynd and added an *a* to make Catalynd.

"Very nice," Benton said. "I like the story of your name."

"Yeah, thanks. I do too."

"Benton," Buddy asked, "are you enjoying yourself?"

"Yes, I am. I really am."

JUNE

. . . in the trees . . . forms of the trees . . . silent, in trunk and myriad-angles of branches . . .
. . . in the woods . . . very pleasant . . . all Nature so calm in itself, the early summer grass so rich, and the foliage of the trees . . .

—*Specimen Days* by Walt Whitman

Catalynd was glad it was the beginning of June. She regularly sketched with Benton, and this time of year was an excellent time to draw the vibrant green leaves and grass. She and her artist friend were stationed in front of a tree that had been broken in half. The top half of the tree now rested on the ground. "Look, the moss on its trunk looks like a green dress, and the ferns on its sides look like a fancy coat," she said. He nodded.

Catalynd turned to the bottom half of the tree, which had survived the car slamming into it. She studied its shape, its injured sides and ragged crown. It reminded her of a form she'd seen recently. She squinted to try to remember. It escaped her, so she returned to her sketching. A few moments later, her head shot up. "I know." The girl took out her phone and brought up the image that had finally come into her mind. "Yes." She passed it to Benton, who nodded again. "It looks like the tree in van Gogh's *Starry Night*."

They were sitting at the edge of the Sourland Mountain Preserve. Catalynd had walked to the tree from the car, carrying her supplies. She had opened her folding chair and positioned it in front of the tree that had broken her legs. That had been *big*. It had been eight months since she had gotten out of the wheelchair, and yet the experience was still a daily presence in her mind.

Her mom had suggested that Cat and Benton go to the Preserve that morning. It was her mom's first day to volunteer in the Preserve garden. "It could be a kind of therapy for you to see the tree and be in front of it and draw it. I think for me it'll be good therapy taking care of the garden."

Cat wasn't convinced it was a good idea for her. She had been to the Preserve many times. She and Hattie and Gwilym often rode their bikes on the trails; she and her family had taken many walks here. *But this is different. What if I have a panic attack, like Mom did in the car? What if I pass out or get sick? What if seeing it gives me depression?*

Benton had said, "I think it is a good idea. If it makes you uncomfortable, we can walk on the trails. You might be surprised by your reaction to finding and sitting in front of the tree."

And so Cat agreed, and here they were. The tree had not been hard to find. There were faint tread marks on the road leading to the damaged tree. Where they parked the car was about five minutes from the spot. The park was dense with trees, vibrant in their summer greens. The sunlight shone through the branches. Cat thought it was making a path for them to their destination. She held her folding chair in one arm and her board, sketching pad, and bag of pencils in the other.

When she came upon the tree, she saw that the standing part of it was leaning back, forced into the position by the impact of the hit. From the road, the severity of the bend had not been visible. With this angle and the fallen trunk flat on the ground, it looked like an arrow marking the whole horrible experience. The sight hit Cat's chest like a heavy rock. She stood and looked at the scene for a time while deciding whether to set up her work-station. She wasn't sure if she wanted to proceed.

"Cat?"

"Yes?"

"Are you going to set up your station?"

"Yes, Benton."

"Okay. I'm going to go over here a ways so you can have your space." He moved off to her right. She listened to his boots crunching the branches and leaves.

Cat blinked her eyes to keep back tears. Her heart pounded. She slowly put down her bundle and sat cross-legged in front of the tree. *I'm sorry. I didn't mean to hurt you. To break you in half like that. Even though I wasn't the one who hit you.* She crossed her arms over her knees and rested her head on them. It felt good—the tears on her cheeks and the surge of emotion she felt. She looked up at the tree. "You broke once, but I have been broken two times." Cat stretched out her legs. "But they're good now." She rubbed them. "I guess no one can fix you . . . But you look all right."

She set up her area to sketch. Inside her pencil bag was a package of tissues her mom must have put in there. She blew her nose and wiped her eyes—she was ready to draw.

A while later, she heard someone approaching her from behind. Benton was still off to her right. She turned around to see a little girl on a silver tricycle. She was wearing a pink unicorn helmet. It included a rainbow Mohawk. "Your helmet's very cool."

"Thank you." The girl rocked her handlebars back and forth. "Why are you drawing that tree?" Her parents rode up behind their daughter.

Cat wasn't sure if she should explain, especially since the child's parents were with her.

"There's a broken tree back there." The child turned her head, and the rainbow Mohawk shined. "There are flowers growing out of its head."

"What color are the flowers?" Cat asked.

"Yellow!" She started backing up her bike. "Well, gotta go. Bye."

"Bye," Cat said. She watched the girl turn around. "You're good at that."

"Thanks."

Benton was standing next to Cat. "There's another tree like this one back on one of the trails," she told him. "There are yellow flowers growing from its head."

"We should go find it."

"Not today," Cat said. "I want to sit here with this tree. My tree. I'm going to come and visit it often."

❧

But there is every kind of wound in every
part of the body.

—*Specimen Days* by Walt Whitman

GLOSSARY

Acrylic paint: a permanent paint, applied with a brush or palette knife; may be thinned with turpentine

Anxiety: a mental health disorder that causes worry, apprehension, fear, and even panic attacks; alters a person's thoughts and moods; treatable with therapy and medication

Art: objects created purely for aesthetic reasons by human beings to evoke emotions, feelings, and thoughts in the viewer; some people claim that animals have artistic talent, but only humans can make art that expresses ideas or concepts

Art gallery: a place that displays art by an artist or a group of artists, often centering on a style or theme

Art history: the study of culture and style in a historical time or place or within a group of people

Art movement: a style or philosophy of art that is created by a group of artists with a common goal and lasts over a period of time

Art museum: a building that houses works of art and provides education about them

Art period: an epoch with a commonality among artists; includes literature and music

Art style: a recognizable pattern, form, or technique that an artist or group of artists incorporate into their artwork (see Art movement)

Artist: a person who creates art objects, ideas, or concepts for a career or hobby

Benton, Thomas Hart: American painter/muralist, 1889–1975; a Regionalist who portrayed rural American scenes, especially in his paintings from the 1930s; he also painted murals

Brush: a tool used in painting, with different types used for oil, acrylic, and watercolor paints

Canvas: a durable woven fabric stretched over a wooden frame, then painted on

Color: how light is reflected onto an object; has three attributes: hue or tint—the actual color; intensity—degree of purity or strength; value—the lightness or darkness; red, orange, yellow, green, blue, and violet colors are created by light

Complementary colors: the result of mixing two primary colors

Composition: the way elements are arranged in a picture; also applies to writing and music

Depression: a mental health disorder that causes an individual to feel lethargic, hopeless, and sad; can affect a person's thoughts and moods; treatable through therapy and medication

Easel: wooden frame with legs that holds an artist's canvas

Genre: a specific subject matter, such as a still life, landscape painting, or picture depicting the activities of everyday people

Hue: a color or shade; a color's position on the color wheel in relationship to white (see Color)

Impasto: a technique in which a heavy layer of paint is applied with a loaded brush onto a painting, leaving a thick surface when it dries; used by Vincent van Gogh in his paintings

Impressionism: a major art movement begun in nineteenth-century France and characterized by the artists' focus on light and atmosphere in landscape; Impressionists' works were sometimes considered sketches instead of finished works of art; Claude Monet's 1874 painting *Impression, Sunrise* is said to have inspired the movement

Landscape art: a central theme/genre type of painting popular in American art in the mid-nineteenth century; artists include the Hudson River School painters and Georgia O'Keeffe

Medium or media (pl): material such as oil and acrylic paint, marble, metal, wood, video, or a combination of materials called mixed media that is used to make an artwork

Mental health condition: disorder or illness in a person's brain that has to do with the chemicals there; treatable with therapy and medication

The Met: The Metropolitan Museum of Art; an art museum in New York City that holds a collection of art covering more than five thousand years of history; one of the greatest museums in the Western Hemisphere, it attracts a wide variety of people, no matter their knowledge of art or art history

MoMA: The Museum of Modern Art; a leading art museum in New York City devoted to the modern visual arts; contains nearly two hundred thousand works of modern and contemporary art, including van Gogh's 1889 painting *Starry Night* and Monet's *Water Lilies* series painted from 1914–26

Monet, Claude: French painter, 1840–1926; his art captured nature in light and colors; his *Impression, Sunrise* is considered to be the first Impressionist painting

Moses, Grandma: American painter, 1860–1961; untrained painter of rural landscapes capturing an unvarnished view of times gone by; began her career at age seventy-eight and quickly received national attention for her late entry into the art world

Mural painting: a painting on a wall

Oil paint: a type of paint applied with a brush or palette knife

Pastels: medium made of sticks of compressed colored powder; often used on tinted paper

Pennsylvania Academy of the Fine Arts: the oldest art museum and school in the US; founded in 1805 in Philadelphia, it has a large collection of American art and casts of classical sculpture from the Louvre

Perspective: a system that represents three-dimensional space on a two-dimensional surface so that an object in the background appears smaller than one in the foreground

Point of view (POV): from where, or the location of where, the viewer observes an artwork

Portrait: a picture of a person or an animal; may be a painting, photograph, or collage

Primary colors: red, yellow, blue; colors not made by mixing other colors

Printmaking: the act of transferring an image onto paper or fabric using any number of different techniques, such as screen printing or etching

Radio dramas: dramas performed by well-known actors and produced for radio listeners from the 1940s to the 1980s; included comedy, horror, mystery, detective, and sci-fi

Sculpture: a three-dimensional work of art made of various materials, such as bronze or wood

Secondary colors: colors made by mixing primary colors, in particular orange, green, and purple/violet

Shade: a color made by adding black to make it darker; areas of a picture that represent an absence of light

Sourland Mountain Preserve: four thousand acres located on Sourland Mountain in central New Jersey with a rich diversity of plant and animal life; offers hiking, biking, horseback riding, and bird-watching

Sketch: marks made on paper with a pencil or pen or other held instrument; a drawing, painting, or model made as a rough draft for the final work of art

Still life: a painting that is usually of objects arranged on a tabletop, such as flowers in a vase; emerged as an independent subject in the sixteenth century

Studies: a sketch or drawing done in preparation for the main piece of art, usually for a painting (see Sketching)

Tint: a color made by adding white to make it lighter (see Color)

Turpentine: a substance used to thin acrylic paint or to clean brushes

Values: the lightness or darkness of a color (see Color); Monet's work captures the atmosphere in a landscape by using values of color

van Gogh, Vincent: Dutch painter, 1853–90; a major artist who used pure, intense color and thick brushwork called impasto; although still popular today, he allegedly he sold only one painting during his lifetime; he lived with depression

Viewfinder: an instrument that assists an artist in cropping a scene to create a composition

Visual arts: forms of art, such as painting, sculpture, photography, and drawing

Whitman, Walt: American writer/poet/publisher/printmaker, 1819–92; a literary icon, his most famous work is *Leaves of Grass*; he visited wounded Civil War soldiers in hospitals, then wrote about his experience in *The Wound Dresser*; he lived with depression

Wyeth, Andrew: American painter, 1917–2009; one of the best-known twentieth-century realistic Regionalists, his most recognizable painting is *Christina's World* (1948)

PAINTINGS

The Old Checkered House by Grandma Moses, 1944

Still Life with Fruit Dish by Paul Cézanne, 1879–80

The Starry Night by Vincent van Gogh, 1889

Homestead by Thomas Hart Benton, 1934

Christina's World by Andrew Wyeth, 1948

RESOURCES

The Arts: A Visual Encyclopedia

Gardner's Art through the Ages: The Western Perspective

Janson's History of Art: The Western Tradition, 8th edition

Andrew Wyeth: People and Places

Complete Prose Works Specimen and Collect, November Boughs and Goodbye My Fancy by Walt Whitman (Kindle edition)

Walt Whitman's Leaves of Grass, The First (1855) Edition, edited with an introduction by Malcolm Cowley (Penguin Classics, 1986)

The Wound Dresser, A Series of Letters Written from the Hospitals in Washington During the War of the Rebellion, by Walt Whitman (Small, Maynard & Co. 1898, reprinted by University Libraries, University of Colorado at Boulder)

The Portable Walt Whitman, edited with an Introduction by Michael Warner (Penguin Classics, 2003)

Walt Whitman, Words for America, by Barbara Kerley, illustrated by Brian Selznick (Scholastic Press, 2004)

Poems by Walt Whitman (Kindle edition)

The Wound Dresser: A Series of Letters Written from Hospitals in Washington During the War of the Rebellion by Walt Whitman (Kindle edition)

Leaves of Grass by Walt Whitman (Kindle edition)

ORGANIZATIONS

International Foundation for Research and
Education on Depression (iFred)
P.O. Box 17598
Baltimore, MD 21297
http://www.ifred.org

Hope for Depression Research Foundation
40 West 57th St., Ste. 1440
New York, NY 10019
(212) 676-3200
https://www.hopefordepression.org

Mental Health America
500 Montgomery St., Ste. 820
Alexandria, VA 22314
(703) 684-7722
(800) 969-6642
http://www.mentalhealthamerica.net

National Alliance of Mental Illness (NAMI)
3803 N. Fairfax Dr., Ste. 100
Arlington, VA 22203
(703) 524-7600
Help Line (800) 950-6264
https://www.nami.org

Depression and Bipolar Support Alliance (DBSA)
55 E Jackson Blvd., Ste. 490
Chicago, IL 60604
(800) 826-3632
https://www.dbsalliance.org

ACKNOWLEDGMENTS

Norman Maclean wrote in his acknowledgments for *A River Runs Through It* that "Although it's a little book, it took a lot of help to become a book at all." And so, first off, I write that I am beholden to my friends for their encouragement and enthusiasm: Barbara White, Ron White, Germaine Van Zutphen-Ameye, Patricia Brother, Michelle Bowen, and Marc Croteau. I am grateful for my dear friend Abbie Møgelvang, who became my very first editor. I thank my family for their support: Mom, Dad, Cheryl, and Amy. I am appreciative of the early readers of my manuscript: Adrian Fogelin, Amy Cleverly, Ann McCullen, and Dr. Taylor Hagood, Professor of English, Florida Atlantic University. I say cheers to my main reader, Natalie Anne Stocky. The great work of my second editor, Gina Hogan Edwards, remains immeasurable to my writing. And thank you, Clete Barrett Smith, my editor, for your clear and concise advice. I sought expertise on mental health issues and art history knowledge from: Heather Carr, Psychiatric Nurse Practitioner; Dr. Huda Akil, Professor of Neurosciences, Department of Psychiatry, University of Michigan; Lorena Bradford, Head of Accessible Programs, Education Division, National Gallery of Art; Janice Machin, Adjunct Professor of Art History, University of North Florida; Dr. Elizabeth Heuer, Assistant Professor of Art History, University of North Florida; Dr. Kathleen Foster, the Robert L. McNeil, Jr., Senior Curator of American Art, and Director, Center for American Art, Philadelphia Museum of Art; and Jessica Todd Smith, the Susan Gray Detweiler Curator of American Art and Manager of the Center for American Art, Philadelphia Museum of Art. Finally, I feel very lucky to have found Girl Friday Productions. For all their excellent work, guidance, and support, I thank Christina Henry de Tessan, Alexander Rigby, Georgie Hockett, Paul Barrett, Sharon Turner Mulvihill, and Kristina Swarner.

ABOUT THE AUTHOR

Before becoming a full-time writer, Kristin McGlothlin worked at the Norton Museum of Art, where she created and taught art classes. She has a BA in Art History, and a BA and MA in English. Her MA thesis was on the author/illustrator Edward Gorey. McGlothlin wrote and made the artwork for the children's picture book *Andy's Snowball Story* about the contemporary artist

Andy Goldsworthy. *Drawing with Whitman* is her debut middle grade novel. It is the first book in a four-book series titled *Sourland Mountain Series.* A writer since she was thirteen, only now, like a *million* years later, has she settled upon it as her career. She lives in Jupiter, Florida.